There was no right or wrong—only Ben

Dani had spent months imagining seeing him again. Now he was here.

Through the pounding of her heart she felt his arms close tight around her, felt her suddenly defenseless body helplessly clenched to his. This ecstasy and joy and rapturous passion in each other's arms hadn't changed.

She tried to regain control. "I shouldn't be here. I shouldn't be doing this." Dull red color stained her face.

His arms slackened their hold, his hands caressed her back. "Why?" he asked shakily. "There was a time when I lived only for you. But you left me. All these years I've never known why. Tell me now."

She turned her face away to avoid his eyes. There was no way to explain it, to make him understand. She didn't even understand it herself....

MAURA McGIVENY describes herself as an ordinary housewife living in a Detroit suburb with her husband and two sons. In fact, she's a talented author who introduces her readers to faraway places, fascinating characters and intriguing situations. By following the advice of a creative writing teacher she once had, she grabs her readers and makes them experience the world she's created.

The Right Time

Maura McGiveny

Harlequin Books

TORONTO • NEW YORK • LONDON
AMSTERDAM • PARIS • SYDNEY • HAMBURG
STOCKHOLM • ATHENS • TOKYO • MILAN

Original hardcover edition published in 1986
by Mills & Boon Limited

ISBN 0-373-02781-8

Harlequin Romance first edition August 1986

For the man in my life
because he believes in me

Printed in U.S.A.

CHAPTER ONE

DANIELLE stared at the stark white wall in the hospital waiting-room without really seeing it. Her thoughts were trying to scatter in a hundred different directions at once and her emotions were running riot. Guilt swirled through her, and anger and denial, but most of all she felt a bitter helplessness.

Why hadn't she come home sooner? Why hadn't she settled her differences before she left, instead of letting them stand between them like a great dark wall? If the worst happened and she never saw her mother again, she didn't want to be haunted by the memory of all the unspoken words that would never have a chance to be said.

'Here, Dani,' her mother had smiled bravely on her way to surgery. Taking off her wedding ring, she had slipped it on Danielle's finger. 'I want you to have this in case I don't make it.'

Danielle's heart had fallen down to her shoes when she looked at the thin gold band that was still shiny after all these years. 'Oh, Mum. Open heart surgery isn't the risk it used to be.' She had tried to sound reassuring. 'The doctor said he doesn't expect any complications. You'll be well again in no time.'

The pulse of one of Perth's finest hospitals throbbed with life all around her, but Danielle wasn't aware of it. All she could see and hear was her mother. She wrapped her arms around herself, pushing to her feet, and began pacing back and forth trying not to think.

'I have to have a bit of surgery next week, dear,' her mother had said. 'Will you come?'

She remembered the tinny voice coming down through the long distance wires. She wanted to give a hundred excuses why she couldn't, but in the end she couldn't say no. She had to come back. It was always that way.

Echoes of her childhood throbbed at her temples. 'Your brother's having trouble with his schoolwork, dear. Will you help him?' or 'Your sister wants to go to the dance with Jack tonight, but she forgot she told Mrs Radnor she'd babysit for her two little ones. Will you sit for her instead?' or 'Mr Evans' dog needs to go to the vet's and he has no way of getting there. I told him you'd be happy to take him.'

It didn't matter that Danielle might have plans of her own. She was the eldest of the

Williams' three children and she was reliable. Everybody could count on her. Total strangers could count on her. 'Danielle will do it for you,' was a favourite expression of her mother's. From the time she was sixteen, no matter what, no matter where, Danielle did it.

Until Ben Harper.

That was the final straw. Don't think about it, she told herself. Mum was right. It wouldn't have worked out. Look at how soon he married Libby after . . .

Tears gathered in her throat and she savagely swallowed them back. That's all she needed, to be thinking about Ben at a time like this. She'd stand here weeping like an idiot and they would all think she'd gone off the deep end for sure. With an effort, she pushed his memory into some dark corner of her mind and tried to concentrate instead on why she was here. Her mother needed her.

'Coffee, Dani?'

She looked at the paper cup her sister held out to her. 'Thanks, Renee.' Coffee was the last thing she wanted, but she took it and tried to drink it without choking.

Renee's generous mouth curved in a rueful smile when she caught the bright glint of their mother's ring on Danielle's finger. 'Still falling for her old tricks, I see.'

'Old tricks?' Her eyes widened and her head came up with a jerk. She looked at her sister and suddenly really saw her for the first time since she had flown in from Sydney late last night.

At twenty-three, Renee was two years younger than Danielle, but they both shared the same plain features and dark brown hair and clear green eyes. Renee was pleasantly plump, the contented wife of Jack McLeod and the proud mother of two darling boys. Danielle was painfully thin in comparison, almost gaunt, and still very obviously single.

Renee's lip curled at Danielle's look of bewilderment. 'Mum always knew all the right buttons to push to get you to see things her way, didn't she? Like her giving you that ring this morning and saying she might not make it. Don't you think it strange that she didn't give it to Daddy instead of you?' She didn't wait for Danielle's answer. 'Emotional blackmail, that's what it is. She wants you to feel guilty. So here you are, playing right into her hands, pacing the floor, wondering how you could have been so mean to stay away so long, and how you could have left your poor old Mum when she needed you.'

Danielle could only stare at her.

'I'm not saying her operation isn't serious,' Renee went on. 'I was there when the doctor made her see there was no alternative. But Mum wants you to come back home, you know. She still hasn't forgiven you for leaving her.'

'But I had to go,' she whispered helplessly.

'You don't have to tell me that. I knew it was inevitable. I just couldn't figure out why you didn't do it sooner.'

Old habitual guilt stabbed at Danielle. 'Oh, Renee, maybe I should have tried harder to be the daughter she wanted me to be.'

'You had to be you,' she soothed, putting her arm around her and patting her on the back. 'Who can fault you for that? Mum was trying to make you an extension of her, that's what was wrong. Haven't you finally come to see that after these past six years of solitary confinement?'

'Mum thought she knew what was best for me,' Danielle said softly. 'I just didn't appreciate it. And it wasn't solitary confinement.' Her voice rose. 'I met a lot of people and made a lot of new friends.'

'And pigs fly,' Renee scoffed, dropping her arm and stepping back with exasperation. 'Mum showed me all your breezy letters. You might have fooled her, but you never fooled me. I could hear the desperation you tried to hide under all the flowery descriptions of the places you'd been and people you'd seen. You were dying to come back, weren't you? But you couldn't because of Ben Harper.'

'Renee, please.' She quickly glanced at the others in the waiting-room, hoping they hadn't heard. Her father was staring out the window, his hands in his pockets idly jingling some coins. Seated some distance away was her brother, Tom, thumbing through a magazine while moodily drawing on his unlit pipe. Tom's wife, Josie, was madly knitting a shawl in the most outrageous colours imaginable. They clashed, but somehow they all went together as well. There were several other people waiting for their relatives in surgery, but none of them seemed interested in their conversation. 'I don't want to talk about Ben,' she said flatly.

'You're going to have to sooner or later.' Renee's expression softened, but she continued to hammer away at her. 'Mum wants you home again and if she talks you into staying, it's something you'll have to face.'

'I'm not coming home to stay.' Danielle turned away and gripped her hands tightly together, nearly spilling coffee all over before she set the cup down. 'I'm going back to Sidney as soon as Mum's well.'

'Running away never helped anything, you know. All it does is postpone the inevitable.

Good Lord, you loved the man, Dani, but Mum stepped in and put a stop to it. You left him without any real explanation. Do you think I can't tell it's still eating you up?'

'It's not,' she lied, trying to clutch at her rapidly diminishing self-control. 'I got over Ben Harper a long time ago.'

Renee's eyebrows rose. 'If that's the case, then why aren't you a starving artist here in Perth instead of starving in Sydney, making sure the whole width of the country stays between you?'

'I'm not starving,' she said softly. 'I've had a lot of odd jobs in between selling my paintings. I'm doing just fine. Besides, I like it in Sydney.' Her voice became almost apologetic, wishing it was true. 'Everybody who goes there likes it. People can debate about every other city in Australia, but when they come to Sydney, the argument stops. It's so vital, so lively, so alive!'

Renee held up her hands. 'All right, all right! You don't have to sell me the place. Aside from all its obvious attractions, I still say the only reason you're there is because Ben isn't.'

Turning away, Danielle sank into a chair and knew Renee was right. She was there simply to put as much distance as possible between herself and Ben. Nothing in Sydney reminded her of what a fool she was. She bit her lip, almost making it bleed before Renee's attention was distracted by something Tom was saying to their father. Danielle stared straight ahead unseeingly. Oh, why did she have to be so young when Ben came into her life? Why couldn't she have been older and better able to stand up to her mother? Why couldn't it have been the right time for her? Mrs Williams had been wrong when she told her she was too young to know what love was all about. She *had* loved him. She loved him still.

Ben. Ben. Ben! His name rang in her head as his memory washed over her. He was so handsome. Tall and smiling, he was a man with a mind of his own. There was always something about him that set him apart from the rest, but Danielle was never able to put her finger on exactly what it was.

She had been standing in a crowd of girls when Ben came to her school to visit his brother, John, their maths teacher. Up until that time she thought John Harper was the most gorgeous creature she had ever seen. Like all the other girls in her graduating class, she worshipped him from afar.

Then she saw Ben.

One look was all it took. Something happened inside her. She felt a stab of recognition, as if she had known him all her life, which was strange because she had never met him before. John Harper suddenly became a nonentity. Every other man in the world paled to insignificance. Ben smiled at her and her heart somersaulted and began to bang hard against her ribs. Everything around them receded. He might have been the only other person in the room, so exclusive was her concentration. She couldn't take her eyes off him.

His hair was a dark smooth cap of shining silk against his head. His eyebrows were black and winged and above the right one was a tiny fascinating mole her fingers itched to reach out and touch. And his eyes. Oh, they were beautiful golden eyes. They flashed a sentient message for her alone, and her pulse throbbed and she suddenly felt weak and giddy and boneless.

Why he had singled her out when there were so many other girls falling at his feet, would always be one of life's great unanswerable mysteries. Some of her classmates were quite beautiful and some strikingly attractive. Danielle was plain and skinny, a short gawky adolescent. But still, Ben noticed her. Her! His smile became a wicked grin so full of irresistible charm that she thought she must have died and gone to heaven.

Handsome men didn't just appear like this, certainly not in Danielle's immediate vicinity anyway. But here he was and he was smiling at her.

She could still recall the unbelievable euphoria she felt when he actually asked her out. She didn't remember where they went, but it didn't matter. She was only conscious of him. He stood so tall beside her, making her feel fragile and helpless and delicate. She remembered having to look such a long way up into his eyes, enthralled by the dusky amber colour changing to a brilliant burnished gold full of mystery and promise. Cradling her face in his hands, he placed a gentle probing good night kiss on her trembling mouth. It was so incredibly beautiful and breathtaking that she could only stand there in dazed ecstasy. Then he brought her closer against his body and the warmth of his arms folding her in a searingly sweet embrace spread a flame to all the dark and lonely corners of her heart. She willingly tumbled headlong into love. With him, only him, always him.

Those were the idyllic days when she was young and in love. Ben wove his way into her life, her heart and mind and soul. He was her other half, the vital part that made her whole. The world was hers for the taking. There was

nothing she couldn't do, nothing she couldn't
be. With Ben she had a glimpse of a totally
enchanting world where everything was
possible. He had big plans. Although he
didn't tell her all of them, some of the ones
he shared made her gaze at him in wonder.
They were so grand. Almost too grand.
While he wasn't exactly poor, he didn't have
the kind of money it would take to get him
where he wanted to go but he wasn't going to
let that stop him. Danielle wanted to believe
in him. He was Ben Harper and he loved her.
Someday he would give her the world.

But her mother stepped in.

'He's not the man for you,' she said
forcefully when she realised Danielle was
serious about him.

'But I love him, Mum.'

'Love doesn't put food on the table.'

'We'll manage.'

'He's a poor man. Do you want to end up
like his mother? Old before your time? With
nothing to show for your life except a bunch
of runny-nosed kids who'll never be a credit
to you?'

'He's got a lovely family, Mum, if only
you'd try to get to know them.'

Her lip curled. 'I want more for my
daughter than a man who'll do nothing but
keep you barefoot and pregnant.'

To Danielle's romantic mind that sounded like heaven: to be Ben's wife and the mother of all his lovely children. What more could she want? She could just imagine their tiny little faces, miniature replicas of him, with dark hair and golden eyes. And best of all, she and their children would always be safe, surrounded by the warm cocoon of Ben's gentle love. If she had that, she had everything.

But that was six years ago and she hadn't been able to stand up to her mother then. An anguished sob began to rise in Danielle's throat and she crushed it down at once, forcing her thoughts into other channels. Ben was gone, lost to her, part of her past and he had to stay there. Besides, everything was different now. He probably despised her for the way she ended everything so abruptly without any real explanation. It's over, Ben, she remembered telling him. I don't love you any more . . .

She focused her gaze on the waiting-room door and nearly bolted across the room when her mother's doctor came towards them.

He was a tall, balding man with an affable smile, still dressed in his surgical clothes. 'She came through it beautifully,' he said, with the barest trace of I-told-you-so creeping into his tone. 'There were no was her family but she felt cut off from them, alone, apart. She couldn't find her way back. She was here, but she didn't really belong any more.

Her father and Tom and Josie left the room before Renee hissed loudly, '*Danielle!*'

Startled, she turned back to her, her head jerking up when she caught a stricken look on her sister's face before rapidly losing all its colour. Turning in the direction she was looking, Danielle, too, could only stand there gaping in sudden shock.

Ben Harper was coming down the hall towards them. For one insane moment she wondered if her thinking about him so hard had somehow conjured him up. As far as she could tell, he didn't see her. He looked tense and strained and preoccupied. But there was no denying it was Ben.

He stepped into the waiting room and it immediately began to shrink. The sheer force and power of his personality dominated everything and everyone around him. While he was still tall and broad and handsome, she hadn't remembered him to be so breathtakingly beautiful. At thirty-four, his hair was longer than he used to wear it. Now there were distinguished flecks of silver prematurely glinting in the shiny black silk. He was tanned and fit and there were sun-

complications and I think we've cc
her problem. She shouldn't have any
trouble, but we'll know for sure in th
few days.' He accepted their relieved
you's with a gracious nod and put his
on their father's shoulder. 'I suggest you
your family and have a bite to eat now. S
in recovery and it'll be at least another h
or so before we transfer her to cardiac ca
You'll be able to see her then.'

Mr Williams expelled his breath in a lo
slow sigh of relief and looked at his famil
The strain of waiting all day was beginnin
to tell on all of them. 'Yes, of course, Docto
And thank you again.'

'You're quite welcome.' His smile became
beaming. 'I'll have someone come for you
when she's settled. Until later, then.'

When he had gone, Renee and Tom and
Josie and their father practically fell into one
another's arms, laughing and crying at the
same time.

'She's going to be all right!'
'I was so worried.'
'I knew she'd make it.'
'She's always been a fighter.'

Danielle turned away aware of a stran
ache inside her, a loneliness that had beg
when she left Ben six years ago. It had gr
steadily stronger with the passing years.

scored lines across his forehead and at the corners of his eyes as if he spent a lot of time outdoors and smiling. He still had that tiny fascinating mole above his right eyebrow. His nose was straight, his cheekbones prominent, his mouth a strong sensuous curve surrounded by two laughing brackets.

Looking disinterestedly around the room, he suddenly spotted her and jerked into rigid quivering stillness. Recognition hit him and something leaped in his eyes and after a moment he began to smile.

When she saw his eyes a familiar jolt of feeling shot through her spreading to her arms and legs and making the hair on the back of her neck tingle. She always thought if she saw him again there would be condemnation written all over him, but there was no sign of it. He kept looking at her with a bittersweet smile and she giddily thought it was all happening again just like the first time she met him.

Her breath became swift and shallow while everything else was fading away to nothing. She hadn't forgotten a thing about him. His eyes were still deeply gold and bottomless, almost mesmerizing in their intensity. They drew her to him and told her so much, these twin flames of amber drifting over her before settling on the parted curve of her mouth.

Warmth rippled over her. She swayed slightly and her heart began to pound in her throat. She had the insane desire to throw herself into his arms begging his forgiveness, to know once again the exquisite pain and pleasure of his warm, crushing embrace, to experience the driving mastery of his lips parting hers, tasting his sweetness, exploring his mouth, hearing his murmurs of desire deep in his throat. But she didn't move. She couldn't even breathe. They were in a hospital waiting-room with people all around them. It wouldn't do for her to make an absolute fool of herself in front of an audience.

The silence between them seemed endless. Her mouth was dry and she was trembling violently inside. All the emotions she had dammed up for the past six years were screaming to be released, but they had to be crushed back. She no longer had the right to love him. He was married. He belonged to someone else now. Unwanted memories came rushing in, and an agony of shame and regret began to swamp her.

'Ben!' His whispered name escaped her anyway.

The whole world was wrapped up in that one word and he knew it. He looked at her for one more long moment before a bleakness began to invade his eyes, as if he too remembered everything was over between them. 'Dani,' he murmured, his voice just the way she remembered it; like rich dark velvet. 'What are you doing here? I thought you lived in Sydney now.'

'I do.' She swallowed hard and cleared her throat, trying not to sound so breathless. 'My mother had to have surgery today. I came to be with her.'

'Oh.' His voice became stilted. 'I hope she's all right?'

'Yes.' She knew there was no love lost between him and her mother, but still, she had to admire him for making an effort to be polite. 'The doctor just came and told us she's doing fine.'

He smiled again and it was then that she began to notice other little details about him. His suit was navy blue, impeccably cut to fit the tall lean grace of his body. His shirt was a brilliant white and he wore a yellow tie with a fine blue stripe running diagonally across it. His black leather shoes had tassels on them and were highly polished and made his feet look tiny. An aura of understated wealth surrounded him, one he wore comfortably and took for granted.

Danielle felt distinctly shabby next to him. She was wearing faded jeans and a pale pink blouse that had seen better days. Her shoes needed to be polished and her hair was a straight dark mop on her head in dire need of being cut to some kind of style.

Ben looked every inch the successful businessman, while Danielle felt she might as well hang a neon sign around her neck that said, 'This girl has no class'.

What she was thinking must have shown on her face because Renee rescued her just then, before things began to get awkward.

'Ben Harper! How lovely to see you again after all these years,' she bubbled brightly. 'What brings you here today?'

He dragged his eyes away from Danielle and looked at her as if suddenly remembering where he was, his face once again settling into tense strained lines. 'Libby,' he said quietly. 'She isn't due until next month, but she's having labour pains.'

'Oh. I'm sorry,' Renee gasped, knowing the eighth month was often critical in any pregnancy. 'I hope everything will be all right.'

He nodded numbly and the bleakness in his eyes pierced Danielle's misery. Without stopping to think she put her hand on his arm. 'Wouldn't they let you stay with her?'

He shook his head, impulsively covering her hand with his own. 'Oh, Dani. I feel so helpless!'

The depth of his anguish became hers, making her quiver. If only there was something she could say, something to ease his distress. But there was nothing. She really had no business even being here with him at a time like this. His thoughts were all with his wife, as they should be, and she felt she would only be an unwanted distraction for him. She was torn between doing the right thing, leaving him, and doing what she wanted, staying and sharing with him what had to be the worst time in his life.

In the end Renee decided for her. 'We'll be in the hospital dining-room, Danie. I'll tell Dad you've decided to wait with Ben for a while.'

Danielle nodded and felt Ben gently tugging her hand, taking her with him to a small sofa near the windows where they could sit side by side.

So many times in the past six years she wondered what she'd say if she ever saw him again. Now he was here and she couldn't say a word. All her questions and explanations had no place here. This was no time to tell him she had never stopped loving him and was so full of regrets she wanted to die. Her life was so empty without him. She could just imagine how appalled he'd be if she asked him if he ever thought of her.

He was leaning forward, staring emptily ahead, his face white and strained, and he was crushing her hand in his.

Her mother's ring dug into her fingers, but he wasn't even aware of it so she said nothing, content just to sit beside him hoping her being here helped him in some way.

Time dragged by slowly. Neither of them spoke. The touch of his hands said more than words. She knew she'd always remember his strength and power and gentleness.

When hurried footsteps sounded in the hall, Ben looked up as a tall, heavy-set doctor came towards him. He was dressed in green surgical clothes and his face was weary and grim.

'Congratulations, Ben. You have a son. We've got him in an incubator for now. It looks like he'll be just fine.'

'Libby?' he croaked, unaware of dropping Danielle's hand and getting blindly to his feet.

'It was touch and go for a while, but she never gave up. She's asking for you.'

Ben's shoulders slumped with relief and almost in a daze he followed the doctor out of the room.

A heavy sigh broke from Danielle's lips. It didn't hurt her to know that Ben had forgotten she was there. In a way, it was a just irony. She had walked away from him six years ago without looking back. Now he did the same to her.

But she was glad to see he had become so successful in the intervening years. If anyone deserved wealth and all the status that went with it, Ben did.

Finally her eyes turned away from the doorway and slowly moved around the waiting-room. It was empty now, she realised with a sudden little shock, empty and impersonal. Just like her life since Ben. Sydney had never felt like home to her no matter how hard she tried to make it so. Coming back to Perth and seeing Ben again made her realise it never would be home. She felt she belonged nowhere, to no one.

CHAPTER TWO

IN the three weeks following her mother's surgery, Danielle went through a whole gamut of emotions.

By the end of the first week she stopped expecting to run into Ben every time she turned around. If his wife was still in the hospital, her visiting hours were obviously different from those of cardiac patients. She never saw him, by accident or design, in the corridors or dining-room or parking lot. Then she had to laugh at herself for even thinking she might. Ben must have taken one look at her and realised how far apart they were on the social scale now. There was no way he'd want to see her again even accidentally, let alone seek her out. She didn't know whether to be relieved or hurt.

During the second week she found herself making a daring detour to the nursery each day before visiting her mother. After making sure no one was around, she'd go up to the big window and stand for long minutes with her nose almost pressed against the glass. Every time she looked at this tiny sea of new humanity, she felt something close to awe. What kind of greatness was in store for these little ones? Would one of them one day win the Nobel Peace Prize? Or discover the cure for cancer? Or become a great statesman or humanitarian? With all their lives before them, anything was possible.

She had no trouble finding Ben's son. He was the only one in an incubator. There was the barest hint of dark hair on his head and his little arms and legs were flailing and he was crying. The tiny bones in his chest were rapidly rising and falling with every breath. The nursery sister gently turned him over and began rubbing his back, and although Danielle couldn't hear her, she could see she was crooning to him. In spite of herself, something twisted in her chest. So many times she used to picture herself doing that very thing for her children—and Ben's. She closed her eyes tightly and could almost smell the warm, clean scent of baby powder, feel his tiny fingers trustingly clutching her own, hear the burble of his tiny laugh or the strident demand of his cries when it was time to feed him . . .

By the end of the third week she stopped torturing herself with the yearning to return to those impossible days when Ben had been hers. The man he used to be no longer existed. That much was obvious. She could never stop loving him, but he was different now in so many ways and she knew she had to forget him. It was useless to keep looking back. He was married and he had a son. He lived in a world totally removed from hers and if she entertained thoughts of seeking him out, it would only be to drag him back down to her level. She didn't want that for him. It was time to let him go. She was adult enough now. His memories would be enough for her.

Renee was with her mother when Danielle came to see her this bright day in early June. Three weeks of continually monitored rest had her mother looking almost healthy again. Her skin had lost its bluish colour and she was sitting up in her hospital bed with Janet's wildly coloured shawl around her ample shoulders. Her short dark hair was heavily streaked with white and had been washed and curled this morning and shone like a halo around her head. When she spotted Danielle in the doorway, an abrupt silence descended.

'Hello,' Danielle said brightly. 'Am I interrupting something?'

Renee looked guilty and her mother hurried into speech. 'Not at all. As a matter of fact, we were just talking about you.'

'So I gathered.' She gave them a wry look.

'The doctor just told Mum she could go home tomorrow,' Renee blustered, 'and we were trying to think of a way to talk you into staying instead of going back to Sydney.'

Danielle's smile broadened. 'Why don't you just come right out and ask me?'

That seemed to throw them both and they could only stare at her.

Her mother was the first to recover. 'Do you mean it? You'll stay?'

'Yes, Mum.' She laughed at her expression and sat on the edge of the bed, allowing herself to be swallowed up in a warm, smothering embrace. 'I didn't realise how much I missed all of you until I came home again. So,' she straightened and spread her hands, giving her a full blown smile, 'if you'll have me, I'd like to come home.'

'Oh Dani, that's all I ever wanted.' Her mother's eyes filled with bright tears, but she blinked them away and straightened her shoulders. 'I know there were hard feelings when you left. You blamed me for interfering in your life, but believe me, I only wanted what was best for you. I wanted you to be happy and to have peace.'

'I know.' She took her hand and gently squeezed it, blocking out all thoughts of Ben. 'And I really do appreciate all these handsome young doctors you've been strewing in my path these days, but it's got to stop. I want to come home, but you've got to promise me you'll stop playing matchmaker.'

'All right,' she said softly, biting her lip. 'I'll try.'

Danielle's eyes narrowed. Her mother wasn't usually so meek and humble.

'Tell me, Dani,' she murmured, plucking at the flannel blanket covering her legs, 'do you ever think about getting married and starting a family of your own?'

Danielle looked her straight in the eye. 'Yes I do,' she said steadily, 'and I will, once I find a man to compare to Ben.'

At her mother's sharply indrawn breath she felt a twinge of conscience, but she pushed it aside. It was better to bring him out in the open and clear the air once and for all. When she left six years ago there had been a lot of unspoken bitterness. If she was going to stay, now was the time to get rid of it.

'Oh, Dani, are you ever going to get over him?'

'I don't know,' she said honestly, 'but I'm going to try.' She turned to Renee sitting in the chair on the other side of the bed. 'You told Mum about us seeing him?'

Renee nodded uncomfortably.

Danielle's smile became forced. 'I really loved him, you know, even though you said I was too young to know my own mind. I've thought about it a lot since I saw him again and I've come to the conclusion that we probably weren't meant for each other after all. So maybe you were right. Maybe it wasn't love, on his part anyway, since he married Libby so soon. He looks so prosperous now and I'm glad for him. Who knows, if he'd married me he might never have come this far with his life. I might have held him back.'

'Don't say such a thing! Don't even think it!' Her mother snatched her hand away and glowered at her. 'If anything, you were always too good for him!'

'No I wasn't.' Danielle didn't raise her voice, but it was full of steel and her green eyes were steady. Silence descended between them and when it became deep and humming, she stood and lifted her chin. 'No, Mum, I wasn't good enough.'

A nursing sister came in just then and saw two feverish spots beginning to colour Mrs Williams' pale cheeks. 'Who's upsetting my patient?'

Danielle didn't move.

'We were just leaving,' Renee said hurriedly, throwing her mother a sick smile before coming around the bed to take Danielle's arm in a surprisingly strong grip. 'We'll be back later after you've had a nap, Mum.'

She roughly forced Danielle to the door and once out in the hall, threw an accusing look at her, dropping her arm in disgust. 'How could you even think such a thing, let alone say it?'

'What?' she shrugged.

'You know what. About not being good enough for Ben.'

'Well, it's true.'

'It is not.'

'Renee, please——'

'Oh no you don't,' she cut her off. 'You're not going to make a statement like that and then just let it hang there. I've never heard such rot in my life. Not good enough! Seeing him again did this to you, didn't it? All of a sudden you're Miss Inferiority because he's so well off. You're getting thinner every day and you've got black circles under your eyes from not sleeping and you've been trailing around this hospital for the past three weeks as if your best friend just died. Why, you're even dressed for it.'

Ignoring most of what she said, Danielle helplessly looked down at her jeans and the black turtle neck sweater she had paired with them. 'What's wrong with the way I'm dressed? I'm clean.'

'Of course you're clean,' she said scathingly, 'but you look like you're on your way to a hippie funeral not to a hospital to cheer up your sick mother.'

Her shoulders slumped. Everything Renee said was true and she was suddenly ashamed. 'I'm an ungrateful wretch, aren't I? And selfish to boot.'

'No you're not. You're just a little mixed up, that's all. You need a good talking to and I just gave it to you. Shall we start over?'

Renee meant well, she knew, but it was so hard to let go. 'Oh, Renee, I feel so old. Life has passed me by.'

'Twenty-five isn't old,' she said softly, leading her down the hall and out into the sunshine to where her car was parked. 'You'll feel better once you really put Ben behind you and concentrate on what's ahead.'

'There's nothing ahead.'

'Of course there is. You keep looking at yesterday. That's why you've lost sight of tomorrow.'

She knew Renee was right, but wave after wave of hopelessness rolled over her. She didn't want to stop thinking about Ben. Even this futile longing for him was better than not thinking of him at all.

Renee seemed to understand. 'It's time to let him go, Dani. You can do it if you want to.'

'I'm right back where I started six years ago,' she said hollowly. 'I let Mum talk me into leaving him. It went against everything I believed in but I did it. I told myself she was right. Then by the time I realised I couldn't live with the choice I'd made, he was married. So I left and tried to lose myself in new surroundings. But look at me. Look where it's got me. I'm still not a very good artist and my life's just been one long string of odd jobs. I don't belong anywhere. I thought since Ben has a son now, I'd be able to come back and not have it bother me so much. But it does. Deep down it still does. Oh, why do I have to love him so much?'

Renee expelled her breath on a sharp sigh, not knowing what to say.

'Why can't I forget him?' she flung at her. 'Why is he with me in everything I do? Sometimes I picture him so vividly I can almost reach out and touch him. I think if I turn my head real quick, I'll catch him walking behind me. A hundred times a day I think of things to tell him, things I want to share with him.' Her breath caught on a sob.

'It's not as if you're likely to see him again, you know. He doesn't move in the same circles we do any more.' Her face was full of compassion. 'Maybe coming home is the best thing after all. You'll see that it wasn't meant to be and you won't have to try so hard to forget him. It will simply die a natural death and then you'll be free to love someone else. I know you feel bad right now,' she soothed, 'but you can't change the past, so take a good hard look at it then let it go. Everything's changed at home now anyway. Mum and Dad need you. That's what's different from before. You'll have your hands full if you concentrate only on that.'

Danielle heard her, but it took a few minutes for it to sink in then she slowly turned and gave her a changed look. 'Then it's true? About Daddy's finances? And how he's drinking more than ever to block it all out of his mind?'

Renee nodded miserably. 'He told you?'

'Tom did,' she said flatly. 'He and Josie have been dropping hints all over the place but I thought they were exaggerating. You know Daddy always liked a drink or two before dinner.'

'He drinks a lot more than that now. Haven't you noticed?'

Danielle shook her head. 'I really haven't been home all that much. Between visiting Mum and going out with those poor un-

suspecting doctors she fixed me up with . . .'
Her mouth twisted. 'What happened?'

'Daddy thought he'd dabble in the stock
market—without knowing the first thing
about it,' she said through her teeth.

'Tom said he invested quite a bit?'

'Just his whole life savings, that's all.'

Danielle's eyes widened. 'But that's what
he was going to pay Mum's bills with! And
he was hoping to buy a cottage in the country
when he retired!'

'That's what he always said, but he can
kiss that dream goodbye now. The man he
gave his money to was nothing but a thief.'

'Oh, Renee. What did Mum say?'

'She doesn't know yet, thank heaven. I
don't know when Daddy's going to tell her.
Jack and I are trying to help but we can't do
all that much. And Tom and Josie give what
they can, but it all just seems to go for drink.
That kind of leaves it up to you, doesn't it?'

Danielle took a deep breath and slowly let
it out, trying not to sound as shaken as she
felt. 'I guess it does.' Then she had to smile.
'At least it gives me something else to think
about besides Ben, doesn't it?'

Renee laughed and knew her sister had
come to a turning point. She just might get
over Ben now.

Danielle couldn't stop thinking about her

father all that day and when she got home that evening, she found him sitting morosely in front of the television set, an almost empty whisky bottle on the table beside him. 'Hello, Dad,' she said brightly. 'Sorry I'm late but after I left Mum this afternoon, I went looking for a job.'

His head jerked up in surprise and deep lines began to furrow his brow. 'A job?' he said cautiously, switching off the set before sinking back in his chair.

Her breezy smile was meant to disarm him and coming to his side, she wound her arms around his neck and dropped a kiss on top of his snow white hair. 'When I asked you last night about my coming home to stay, I didn't expect you to have to support me.'

'That's what fathers are for,' he argued softly.

'I'm twenty-five years old now. Isn't it about time I stand on my own two feet?'

'Danielle——'

'I won't pretend I don't know what's happened to your investments,' she cut in, dropping to her knees in front of him. 'Tom told me. And Renee. But that's not the only reason I need a job. I'm used to supporting myself, but I want to help you as well. Is that such an awful thing?'

'You know it isn't.' He looked at her and

ruefully shook his head. 'If only I hadn't been so stupid to think I could get rich quick. I knew your mother was going to have whopping bills with her heart and all, but I wanted to have enough money to be able to send you to art school and to buy a nice little cottage as well. I promised you that much when you were younger and I intended to do it even though you didn't live at home any more. You've got such talent. It's all being wasted.'

'No it isn't,' she argued. 'I had a chance to meet a couple of artists in Sydney and they showed me some things. Believe me, that short time with them was worth at least two years in art school. Besides, I'm not going to give up painting. There'll still be time for it in the evenings after work.'

'What kind of work are you talking about?' he asked quietly, focusing his eyes on her with an effort.

'I put my name in an agency specialising in domestics.'

He frowned.

'You know, housekeeping and the like.'

'Dani!'

'It's what I do best, Dad. I can't type so I'd be no good in an office. And you should see me behind a cash register.' She rolled her eyes and shook her head. 'Hopeless! Besides, what does it matter what I do as long as I do my best?'

He couldn't argue with that but he gave her an unfathomable look. 'What about Ben Harper? Does your running into him again have anything to do with this decision to come back home?'

Her face softened. 'You don't miss a thing, do you?' She got up from her knees and settled herself in his lap, her head nestling under his chin the way she used to do when she was a little girl. 'In a way I guess it does. He's even more gorgeous than I re-membered,' she sighed, her fingers restlessly playing with the buttons on his shirt. 'And I still love him as much as I ever did.' Her face changed. 'But he's different now and I have to accept that he's beyond me. He's married and has a son, so it's all right for me to come back home again. It's not as if I have to worry about seeing him again and eating my heart out for him. Like Renee says, he's sure to be moving in different circles these days.' Maybe if she said it often enough, she'd come to believe it.

Her father's arms came around her gently. 'I always felt I failed you when it came to Ben. Your mother and I should have let you make your own mistakes. I knew you loved him. And he loved you. If ever two people were meant for each other . . .' His mouth twisted. 'I'm really sorry, Dani.'

'I know, Dad. Thank you for that.' She smiled brightly and decided this conversation had gone far enough. 'I read somewhere that everything happens for a reason. Maybe Ben wouldn't have amounted to anything if he'd married me.'

'And maybe he'd be twice as well off.'

'Come on, Dad. You're the one who taught me to think positive.' She slid off his lap and took his hands, coaxing a smile out of him before pulling him up from his chair. 'Did you put that casserole in the oven when you came home from work, like Renee told you to?'

He was weaving on his feet and she knew if she hadn't been here to take care of him, he probably wouldn't have eaten that night.

She settled in and found it surprisingly easy to push Ben to the back of her mind during the long months of her mother's convalescence.

All that winter Danielle's workdays were busy and varied. No job was too big or too small for her. Willing to try anything, she cheerfully scrubbed floors and cleaned house for various housewives, washed walls for an invalid grandmother, catered candlelit meals for a handsome bachelor, who had an extraordinarily large number of girlfriends, and she even held down a gem of a job for two months as a mother's helper for a frail girl in her mid-twenties who, expecting her first baby, was overwhelmed to find she had delivered twins.

Her salary was adequate, her tips more than generous. Without a qualm, she handed the entire sum to her father at the end of each week. At first he didn't want to take her money, but Danielle gently insisted and before too long he came to rely on it.

She was finishing up a month's work as a chambermaid for a large hotel when Christmastime rolled around. She was unusually busy the week before the holiday and she was glad because it kept her from thinking too much. Christmas was always a miserable time for her. She couldn't forget how Ben loved this time of year. Whenever she heard the carols, the memories would swamp her.

He used to love to take her to the brightly decorated malls and spend hours window shopping, looking at all the beautiful things neither of them could afford. Then he'd turn to her and cup her face with both his hands and lightly drop a kiss on her mouth. 'Someday, my love,' he'd say, 'it'll be Christmas and we'll be able to go into any store and buy whatever we want and not have to look at a price tag.'

She'd laugh up at him, carried away by his enthusiasm, but deep down she knew she didn't need this promise of riches. All she needed was him. His love was a rare and priceless thing. But he didn't understand that. Neither did her mother.

'You'll be poor, Dani,' she had told her over and over. 'If you marry him, you'll never have anything. He's a dreamer, not a doer.'

Danielle never could remember when she started believing her mother. She did remember showing her the Christmas gifts Ben gave her. They weren't expensive, her favourite cologne and a delicate porcelain figurine, but they showed his thoughtfulness and sensitivity and they held a special meaning for her. She had to smile, even now, when she remembered they were lovingly tucked away in a drawer in her room.

Mrs Williams' lip had curled as she dismissed them out of hand. 'These are what your fine young dreamer calls gifts? They're an insult to you, but you're too naïve to know it.'

Danielle stopped these thoughts from going any further. They weren't helping anything. All she was doing was making herself miserable. She viciously kicked at a stone in her path on her way to the employment agency and jammed her hands in the pockets of her jeans. Forget it, she told herself. It's over and done with. She chose to leave Ben a long time ago and she had to live with it.

Pulling open the door to the snug little office building, she took a deep breath and forced herself to smile. 'Hello, Miss Higgins. Anything interesting for me today?'

The tall, thin woman looked up from her littered desk and grinned. 'Danielle. You're just the person I wanted to see. I need someone to help Maurice cater a party on Christmas Eve.'

'Oh, Miss Higgins!' Her face immediately fell.

'I know. I know. But I'm at my wit's end. Won't you do it as a personal favour to me?'

'You don't know what you're asking. The man's impossible. He's such a——'

'Now, now. Be nice.'

Danielle gritted her teeth. '——egotistical, supercilious, pompous ass.'

'I told you to be nice.' Miss Higgins shook her head, sighing sympathetically. 'Be that as it may, he's an excellent chef in spite of his personality and he's asked for three extra girls to help with this party.'

'Can't you find someone else?' She sank into the straight backed chair in front of the desk. 'I still wake up nights in a cold sweat remembering how he ranted and raved at me at that Women's Club Tea. I took one look at his goose liver paté and thought somebody got sick on the table. And the fuss he made when I started apologising to all those women and tried to whisk it away before somebody else added to it!' She waved her hands theatrically in the air.

Miss Higgins struggled to contain a grin. Biting the inside of her cheek, she swallowed back a laugh and forced herself to look at Danielle's serious face. 'That's a mistake that can happen to anyone who's not used to delicacies of that kind.'

Danielle shuddered violently. 'Delicacies! I can't imagine anybody actually *eating* something that looks like that!'

Miss Higgins coughed. 'Yes, well ... Maurice is prepared to pay extra since it's Christmas Eve and I'm having a devil of a time trying to find a third girl.'

'What about Janice or Janet?' she asked, putting in a good word for the twins who had worked at the hotel with her for the past month.

'I'm already one step ahead of you. They're the other two you'll be working with. I rang them yesterday and after twisted their arms, they agreed to help me. They offered to drive you there if I could talk you into it. You won't be able to make bus connections that late in the evening.'

'You're all conspiring against me,' she murmured.

'We care about you is more like it. What do you say, Danielle? Will you do it for me? There's nothing else I can offer you right now and I know you can use the money.'

'All right,' she sighed, knowing she really had no choice. Her mother and father were spending Christmas Eve with some people her father knew, and Tom and Renee wouldn't be coming with their families until Christmas Day. She didn't want to spend her time at home alone thinking about Ben. 'But if Maurice has any complaints . . .'

'I'll just sympathise with him and ignore them like I did last time,' she laughed. 'You know you're my most reliable employee.'

CHAPTER THREE

DANIELLE sat in the back seat of Janet's rusty little car, dressed in the uncomfortable black bombazine uniform that was Maurice's trademark. She adjusted the tight, white collar and cuffs and resolutely put Ben out of her mind. It was Christmas Eve and thoughts of him had plagued her all day long. She wished they'd hurry and get to where they were going. Crowds of people always seemed to make it easier for her to forget.

'Look at these houses, will you?' Janet marvelled, driving along the broad streets with fine old lawns and magnificent trees on the sunny coast, south of Perth. 'I wonder what kind of people actually live in them?'

The farther south they drove, the more impressive the houses got. Some were built on rolling landscaped hills offering glimpses of natural wood and stone and wide windows in a variety of architectural styles. The Indian Ocean made a spectacular backdrop shimmering brightly blue in the distance.

'How do you like that one?' Janet pointed to a rambling, grey brick structure sprawled on a low green hill before glancing down to a slip of paper in her lap. 'Can't you just imagine the ocean view from inside?'

'What I wouldn't give to live in it for a week!' her sister sighed.

Danielle could only look at it, her jaw falling open in spite of herself.

It was a beautiful house, understated for all its immense flowing lines, and full of gracious dignity as it stood beneath the bright green foliage of the tall trees surrounding it. The lawns were a long gentle slope of green dappled with sunshine. Low to the ground, a colourful profusion of wild flowers wound their way across the front to give it a homey touch.

She could just imagine the family who lived here: a loving mother and father with at least five or six laughing children and two large collie dogs romping and barking around the flower beds. This was a house that was meant to be a home, full of peace and comfort and gracious hospitality. She could almost hear the soft, murmurous hum of bees and the drowsy rustling leaves in the mellow summer sunshine.

Janet slowed her car and began to turn into the long drive in front of it.

'What are you doing?' Janice shrieked. 'You can't just drive up to a house like this

for a closer look. What if the owner sees us
and has us thrown in jail for trespassing? I
know it's Christmas, but you're expecting a
bit much from the holiday spirit. Besides,
we're late for Maurice's party as it is.'

'Relax,' Janet laughed at her sister. 'We
belong here. This is where the party is.'

She let out a low whistle and shook her
head. 'I don't believe it. This has got to be
the most beautiful house in the world. And
we're actually going to get to see the inside!'

Danielle had to laugh too. For twins, Janet
and Janice were remarkably different. They
looked alike, tall and gangly with coal black
hair and sparkling blue eyes, but their
personalities were so different. Janet was on
the quiet side, introspective and somewhat
aloof, while Janice jumped right in to any
situation with both feet, always saying the
first thing that popped into her head and
living with the consequences afterward. In a
way, Danielle envied her. Janice wasn't afraid
of much, and there was always something
going on around her.

A long line of cars were parked along the
drive and Janet found a place for hers behind
a low red sportscar. 'Would you look at that
beauty!' she said, trying to hide her trepi-
dation as she got out and held the door for
Danielle. She straightened her uniform and

gave her sister and Danielle a critical look before taking a deep breath and leading the way up towards the house. A hot wind was blowing through the trees and the sun was beginning to sink towards the horizon. She hoped it would be cooler inside.

'Whoever the people are who live here,' Janice said softly after a few minutes, 'they're not snobs.'

They were passing everything ranging from a shiny black Rolls Royce to a rusted out Holden.

'Somehow that makes me feel better.' Janet's bright blue eyes were wide with nervousness.

Danielle slowly walked past a few more cars then finally had to laugh. 'Look at us,' she shook her head. 'You'd think we were gatecrashers the way we're acting. Even you, Janice. And I thought you weren't afraid of anything! But here we are, all nervous and twitching at our clothes and straightening our shoulders as if to say we're not really afraid.'

'You mean you're not?' Janet asked.

'Not the way you are. I've got something else to worry about. All I can think of is what Maurice is going to say when he sees me again.'

Both girls looked at her then at each other and then began to laugh, all their unfounded fears deserting them.

'Oh, that's right. The last time you worked for him was at that Women's Club Tea, wasn't it?'

Danielle's face burned. 'Do you think I'll ever live it down?'

'Maybe he'll have forgotten all about it by now,' Janet said sympathetically. 'Goose liver paté. Yuk!'

But when they stepped inside the back door and looked at Maurice's face, it was all too evident that he remembered Danielle vividly.

'*You!*' he said, stunned.

'Hello, sir.' Danielle lifted her shoulders and gave him an impish, if apologetic, smile.

'How could Agatha Higgins *do* this to me?' The rosy little man was wearing a stark white suit to cover his rotund figure. His enormous chef's hat was perched on his head and he put a hand to his forehead, eyeing her with a pained expression. 'I told her I never wanted to see you again.'

'Sorry, sir. Miss Higgins couldn't get anybody else, what with Christmas Eve and all.'

'Why me?' he muttered over and over, shaking his head. 'Why me?'

The three girls silently stood still under a row of gleaming copper pots suspended on a rack from the high ceiling. The kitchen was steamy and full of the delicious sights and smells of Christmas. Soft footed servants dressed in black bombazine uniforms were swiftly moving to and fro, carrying covered silver dishes, tureens, platters and cups. Danielle was dazzled by the fascinating array of exquisite crystal goblets and glasses on the sideboard and the heavy silver trays and snowy white linen. A delicate aromatic broth was bubbling in a huge pot on the stove. Hams were in the ovens and beef roasts, and potatoes were being mashed and mixed with cheese and piped into ornate mounds through a fluted tube before being placed under the grill by three other men in their white chef's garb.

Maurice studied them with his baleful glare until he finally let out a resigned sigh and began barking out orders. 'You're late, but I suppose it's better than not showing up at all. You,' he pointed a stubby finger at Janice, 'straighten your collar and take that tray of canapés to the drawing room and circulate among the guests. And you,' he pointed to Janet, 'take these hot hors d'oeuvres and do the same. Is that dirt on your cuff?'

She looked down at the smudge on her sleeve and hurriedly wiped it at the side of her skirt. 'No, sir.' She took the tray and

quickly followed her sister out before he
could look too closely at it.

When they had gone, Danielle shifted from
one foot to the other in the lengthening
silence. Struggling to find her poise, she
wondered if he was going to dismiss her and
how she was going to get home again at this
time of early evening. She knew she
shouldn't have come. Her black uniform
suddenly felt baggy on her slender frame and
her hair was beginning to loosen from its
braided coil at the back of her neck.
Maurice's unrelenting stare made her feel
more and more awkward and she wondered
how she was going to explain to Miss
Higgins.

Maurice kept looking her up and down, his
dark eyes narrowing and his thin mouth
tightening. 'With a name like Danielle, is it
too much to ask you to behave like your
countrymen and have some reverence for my
food?'

She coloured painfully. She wasn't French.
Her mother just liked that name. 'I really am
sorry, sir.'

'So you said at the time.' One dark
eyebrow arched. 'Well, don't just stand there
like a whipped dog. Take this tray of canapés
and circulate.'

She gulped and nearly slipped on the

highly polished floor in her haste to do as she was told.

Maurice rolled his eyes heavenward as he watched her and sent up a silent long-suffering prayer. 'Why me?' he muttered again.

Danielle quietly left the kitchen, making her way down a long, cool corridor with its floor so shiny it reminded her of a dark mirror. The peace of Christmas was here and just for a moment she let herself think of Ben. She pictured him at home in surroundings like these. She could just imagine all his nieces and nephews coming to visit him and his wife and son in a home like this. He came from a large happy family with a lot of married brothers and sisters. There must be dozens more children born to them in the last six years.

She sighed and stopped outside an open doorway trying not to be dazzled by the colourful sights and sounds of the Christmas party. Her feet sank into a rich dark carpet as she unobtrusively passed through throngs of well dressed, smiling, animated people. There were low carved tables in this room and crystal lamps, silver candlesticks with long red tapers in them, delicate rosewood furniture, ivory-tinted walls and rich, grey velvet draperies at the narrow windows glowing with the last rays of fading sunlight. At the end of the room an enormous Christmas tree sparkled and shimmered with brightly coloured lights and glittering bulbs and slim silvery icicles moving in the slightest breeze. How Ben would love it.

Her circular tray was almost empty ten minutes later when a tall, dark suited man stopped her. She kept her eyes suitably downcast waiting for him to take a canapé and was surprised when his finger came under her chin, forcing her to look up at him.

'Danielle! I thought it was you.'

'Mr Harper!' Her eyes suddenly widened when she recognised Ben's brother.

'What's this Mr Harper stuff? You used to call me John when you finished school and began dating Ben.'

A small helpless laugh stuck in her throat. 'John,' she said shyly. 'Merry Christmas. How are you?'

'Merry Christmas.' His smile was expansive and he waved his full champagne glass absently. 'I'm fine, just fine. And you?'

'Very well, thank you. It's lovely to see you again.' She just had to ask. 'How's Ben?'

'He's doing well, considering.' His look softened and became pensive. 'Haven't you bumped into him yet in this crowd? He said he was going to put in an appearance.' He scanned the room then smiled down at her again. 'He told us he saw you ... about six months ago? At the hospital, right? Your mother had some surgery?'

'Yes, that's right.'

'I hope she's well?'

'Yes.' She didn't want to talk about her mother, but she didn't know how to get him talking about Ben without making it obvious. 'She hasn't had a bit more trouble with her heart. It's as good as new.'

'I'm glad to hear that. And you're looking lovelier than ever.' He stepped back and made a smiling, sweeping assessment of her too slim figure in the awful black uniform, then reached out and clapped his arm around another man's shoulder as he started to pass them. 'Do you remember my brother, Michael?'

Of all Ben's older brothers, she liked Michael the best. He had a zany sense of humour and no matter when she saw him, he always seemed to have a ready smile. He wasn't as handsome as Ben, but he had the same bright gold eyes flecked with darker brown. They were gentle and open and welling with friendliness.

'Hello, Michael.' She transferred her tray to her other hand and held out her right.

'What?' He seemed surprised, looking

down at her. 'A handshake after all this time?' He practically smothered her in a warm, effusive bearhug that made her feel humble and shaken.

How could they be so kind to her after she had treated Ben so shabbily all those years ago? Ben must have told them all about it at the time. She deserved their contempt, not this warm ready acceptance.

A slow mortification began to run through her and she suddenly wanted to be gone from here. How many others of his brothers and sisters were here? She didn't want to see their families and be reminded of all that was lost to her. And she didn't really want to see Ben. Not in a social setting like this. He was bound to be with Libby and she didn't know if she could stand to see him being gently attentive to his wife. She'd never met her, but for years her imagination pictured her as a slim beautiful blonde who had all the social graces Danielle lacked. All at once she was floundering and she felt these two tall men in front of her could see everything she was thinking.

'I really must be getting back to the kitchen,' she said brightly, her throat oddly throbbing. 'It was good seeing you again. Give my best to Ben in case I don't see him.' She turned and blindly made her way through the brilliant sparkling crowd. She had to get out of here. Something painful was opening in her chest. Everything seemed to whirl and dip and plunge and she thought if she didn't hurry, she'd be sick and make an absolute fool of herself.

Once out in the hallway, she took several deep, calming breaths before her eyes fastened on a snowy white chef's suit. Stiffening, she slowly straightened, her eyes moving up from Maurice's rotund waist to his throbbing neck to his livid, purpling face. Her blurred vision suddenly cleared.

'You are not one of the guests!' he said through his teeth. 'How dare you act like one?'

She stared at him with round surprised eyes. Forcing herself to calmness, she swallowed and faced him without flinching. 'I wasn't pretending to be a guest, sir. Those two men were friends of mine. I haven't seen them in a long time and when they stopped to talk to me, I couldn't be rude and not speak to them.'

'Is there some problem, Maurice?'

The dark velvety voice she least wanted to hear came from behind her, shattering the air and making her quiver so much that the heavy silver tray wobbled in her hands before flipping over and falling on to the shiny floor with a loud twanging crash that swirled faster and faster in an ever-closing circle echoing over and over for a good half a minute.

If Maurice was upset before, it was nothing to what he was feeling now. His face became thick and furrowed and flushed. His eyes were bulging and he was almost panting, ready to explode. Icy drops of sweat appeared on his forehead and knotted veins were standing out in his neck. Clenching his fists at his sides, he controlled himself with difficulty and after a moment said in a strangled voice, 'I will handle it, Mr Harper.'

Danielle automatically got down on her knees trying to retrieve the tray and clean up the gooey canapés splattered all over the floor when Ben reached out to stop her.

'Don't, Dani. We'll get someone to clean it.'

'Please, Ben. Just go away,' she said tightly, not daring to look at him. Heavy hurrying footsteps came closer followed by gasping murmurs then a heavy hushed silence. She was suddenly surrounded by a sea of legs and there she knelt, the centre of attention, yet very much alone. The party guests must have heard the commotion and came to see what it was all about.

'How dare you talk to my client like that!' Maurice interjected wildly, ignoring their audience.

Danielle stopped dead. Still kneeling, her head jerked up to Maurice's shocked face then ice slithered down her spine as she slowly turned to look up at Ben.

My client? The words began to bang in her head. *My client!*

She was stunned. Her face paled and she quickly averted it. All her breath left her in a rush. This was Ben's party. Ben's home! And here she was, the incompetent servant, kneeling at his feet in utter shame for all to see. Her humiliation was complete now.

'You will leave this instant,' Maurice grated. 'And I will make sure you never have the opportunity to disgrace anyone again.'

Her first reaction was to apologise, to plead with him for her job. She needed to work. She needed the money. Her father was counting on her. But with Ben standing there, and all his guests, she couldn't say a word.

Slowly getting to her feet, she clasped her hands tightly together to keep them from shaking and straightened, facing Maurice with her chin lifted much too high. 'Yes, sir,' she said quietly. Without really looking at him, she sent a stiff little nod in Ben's direction and turning, started for the kitchen. She couldn't quite muster up enough courage to leave by the front entrance in a final act of childish belligerence.

'Dani, wait.'

Ben's voice stopped her, but she didn't turn around. Helpless tears were beginning to stand in her eyes and she had to keep blinking them back so they wouldn't fall.

He murmured soothingly to his guests that everything was under control. 'Go back to the party,' he was saying. 'I'll take care of this.'

Then she heard Maurice snapping orders to her hapless friend, Janet, to stop gawking and start cleaning up the mess.

Ben came over to her and took her elbow. 'Dani.'

'Please leave me alone,' she choked, keeping her face turned away, wanting to walk away from him with her rags of dignity still intact.

'No. You can't leave like this. Come with me.'

'Ben, please,' she insisted.

He didn't listen. Taking her by the arm, he drew her resistingly across the hall to a wide door and forced her inside before closing it. Then he leaned back against it with his arms folded across his chest.

He stood for a long moment, looking down at her in silence, his burning eyes full of some nameless emotion moving from her pale face to her bedraggled hair loosening from its braided coil, to her hands tightly clenched in front of her shapeless black uniform.

White and tense and rigid, she stared back at him in his expensive black tuxedo with the dark red cummerbund circling his narrow waist.

There was only silence between them, stretching endlessly, lengthening and becoming deep and charged and ringing. Then everything began to fade away: who she was, where she was, what had just happened. There was only Ben. After all this time, there was Ben. She had spent months imagining seeing him again. Now he was here and she couldn't move. She couldn't breathe. Everything she ever thought of saying suddenly deserted her.

It was wrong for her still to be so attracted to him. He was another woman's husband. But she could not drag her eyes away from his face with its strong angular planes and unconsciously sensual lips and piercing golden eyes. Some irresistible force sprang from her body to his, primitive and urgent and overpowering, driving out all logic and sanity. There was no right or wrong here. There was only Ben. Her Ben. The man she never stopped loving. A dreadful yearning came over her, welling up and roaring with passionate fury, choking her throat. She tried to swallow it back but couldn't.

Then she saw him move. Through the pounding of her heart she felt his arms close tight around her, felt her suddenly boneless body helplessly clenched to his. His mouth was on hers, gentle at first, brushing back and forth, then becoming hard and hungry and seeking. His body strained against her. His stirring hardness made her overwhelmingly aware that she wasn't alone in this need to be as close as they could be.

She responded as dry wood to flame. Tears filled her eyes, squeezed through her closed lashes and slid down her cheeks. Her lips were parted and glowing, giving him back kiss for kiss. Her arms came up around him and she clung shamelessly, her body melting into his until she was swept away on a great, golden, roaring tide of love and desire. His hands followed the length of her spine, arching her hips against his, moving in slow unthinkingly rhythmic motions.

He murmured something inarticulate in a thick hoarse voice and she murmured in return. She didn't understand what he was saying, but it didn't matter. His heart spoke for him with violent pounding throbbing urgency.

It was always this way, this remembered ecstasy and joy and rapturous passion in each other's arms. It hadn't changed in six years.

Ben's love still had the power to make the whole world suddenly come alive for her. He was the master, she the pupil. He brought her to bursting, glorious life. In his arms her existence was no longer barren, but shining and endless and full of hope and promise. He was the part of her she thought had been lost forever, the vital part that made her whole.

Her heart was drumming in her chest at the intimacy of their embrace. His fingers spread across the small of her back, moving on her, cupping her, melting in their warmth, making her throb with desire. Her hair broke from its coil and he moved his cheek and jaw in the heavy brown mass, pressing his mouth to it, saying her name over and over.

There was a stricken quality in the sound, an anquish that reached her and she suddenly thought of Libby and then everything began to change. Something in her shrivelled. She wanted to touch him, be touched by him, to hold him and let nature take them where it would but she wasn't totally shameless.

With a small cry, she disentangled her legs from his and broke away from him, raggedly panting, her eyes wide and distended. Still facing him, bending forward from the waist with her fists clenched, she tried to regain her control. 'I shouldn't be here,' she said almost inaudibly. Dull red colour ran up her neck and stained her face. 'I shouldn't be doing this.'

'Oh yes you should,' he whispered, taking a step closer.

She shrank back.

'Don't back away from me, Dani. You don't really want to. I thought everything ended between us six years ago, but God help me, just now I felt how alive it still is, no matter what you say!'

The sight of his tormented face was almost her undoing. 'All right, Ben,' she admitted, 'I won't deny it. You know I never stopped loving you but——'

At once the distance between them closed. He reached out and swept her back into his arms, blindly spurning all her objections.

'Ben!' His name was lost in the wild storm of his kiss.

This is wrong, she thought achingly. She had no right to love him. There were others to consider now, his wife and son. But, oh, for the moment this was heaven. Her hands were clenched in his hair, twining through the thick black silk, mindlessly moving to stroke his ears and neck and the fine fabric of his shirt and the warm bunching muscles she knew were beneath it.

His mouth was warm and firm and opened

wide, covering hers. His tongue touched hers as it never had before. He probed and stroked, drawing a shuddering response from her that made her fingers sink into him and her knees almost buckle. *This* wasn't the same as six years ago. He had refined his way of loving, become more adept, and she was totally captivated, breathlessly immersed in everything he was making her feel. His tall hard body wrapped around hers, fitting to her slenderness perfectly as if they were two halves of a whole.

But this is wrong. The thought intruded again. We shouldn't be here—doing this.

Almost as if he read her mind, his mouth suddenly gentled and his arms slackened their hold, his hands haltingly caressed her back through the black dress for long minutes and then he lifted his head and opened his eyes and looked down at her. Gold fires were slowly being banked there and a heavy flush ran over his face. 'Dani,' he said so quietly she wanted to cry. 'Dani.' He looked long and intently at her, smoothing her wild hair away from her face over and over. 'There hasn't been a single moment these past six years when I haven't dreamed of holding you, kissing you, loving you. It was an ache eating away inside me.'

Then he took her hand with a curious expression and led her to sit beside him on a long dark brown leather sofa.

CHAPTER FOUR

IT was then that she saw she was in a study, its proportions and austerity at once disconcerting her. Innumerable books lined one wide wall from floor to ceiling. There was a large desklike table at one end with a high-backed leather chair behind it. Two plush brown leather chairs were grouped in front of it. Set beside huge windows with a panoramic view of manicured lawns sloping down to the ocean, it was uncluttered, with only a telephone and a small brass lamp on its surface. The floor was like dark polished glass.

At the other end of the room, where they were sitting, a sofa and two more leather chairs were grouped around a low intricately carved wooden table set on an Oriental rug. There were several oil paintings in heavy gilt frames on the panelled walls. Ordinarily the artist in Danielle would have been curious to see who painted them and what the subject matter was, but she barely glanced at them before turning back to Ben, quickly averting her eyes, not wanting him to see the awe she couldn't hide.

This wasn't the Ben Harper she fell in love with all those years ago, she told herself. He was different now. He had gone on, grown, while she stayed the same. His lifestyle was totally removed from hers. His obvious wealth made her uncomfortable, and she trembled awkwardly, jerking to her feet, trying to keep her voice from shaking. 'I really must go.'

'No, Dani,' he said softly, standing beside her. 'Not yet.'

She swallowed past the hard lump in her throat and unwillingly looked into his piercing eyes, wringing her hands. 'What do you want of me?'

'That's a curious thing to say.' His voice was cool with a sudden steely quality she had never heard before. She noticed, too, he was controlling himself with difficulty. 'I never wanted anything from you. But I'm ready to give you anything you ask for.'

'Oh, don't, Ben. Don't even say such a thing. I gave up the right to hear you say that a long time ago.'

'Why?' he asked shakily. 'There was a time when I lived only for you. But you left me. Why did you do it? All these years I've never known why. Tell me now.'

Her chin dipped and she turned her face away to avoid his eyes. There was no way to explain it, to make him understand. She didn't even understand it herself. She never could remember exactly what it was her mother said that finally made her decide to leave him. And anyway, it didn't matter any more. Everything was different now. 'I'm sorry,' she whispered. 'I never wanted to hurt you.'

'That doesn't answer the question.'

She shook her head helplessly and found herself looking at him again even though she didn't want to. 'I don't know why! And anyway, this isn't the time or the place to be having this conversation.'

Tension vibrated all around her. Surely someone must have told Libby what had happened by now, if she hadn't seen it for herself. She was probably looking for her husband and wondering how he could be so rude to their guests. If she came looking for him, she could just imagine the awkward explanations he'd have to make.

'Your guests must be wondering where you are,' she choked.

'They aren't my guests,' he said coolly, looking straight into her eyes. 'They're my mother's. Don't you remember how she always enjoyed Christmas? I told her this year shouldn't be any different from before. I think everybody she ever knew is here.'

An odd mixture of confusion and relief and

regret rippled through her and her widening eyes couldn't leave his face. 'Then you mean this isn't your house? It's your parents'?'

Somehow that made her feel better. He didn't live like this. He was still Ben after all. She knew his parents weren't wealthy, but maybe they'd had some unexpected windfall since she last heard about them. She was happy for them, yet at the same time she felt a small regret for Ben because she knew this was what he always wanted.

'The house belongs to me,' he said, frowning at the changing expressions on her face. 'My mother and dad came to live here when he retired two years ago.'

'Oh.' She came back to earth with a bump and swallowed hard, nervously shifting her glance away from him before saying in a rush, 'It's very beautiful.'

His head tilted, as if her reaction puzzled him. 'It's very empty.'

She sucked in a quick breath and held it, not knowing what to say. That sounded as if he was having trouble with his marriage and if that was true, she was the last person who should know about it. Her heart started to drum in her ears. Her breathing became swift and shallow and involuntarily her eyes flew back to his.

There was a deep sadness there and lines of strain in his face. He was thinner than she remembered, his tall frame not quite so muscular. His hair was more flecked with silver and hollows were beginning to appear beneath his cheekbones.

A shivering sensation started to swamp her but she resisted it. It would be all too easy for her to become an 'other woman' in his life. She loved him enough to want to ease whatever sorrow might be haunting him but it was wrong. She couldn't do that to Libby no matter how much she was tempted to forget all about her. A hazy image of a beautiful blonde woman flashed in her mind again and she immediately turned away. She'd never met Libby. She didn't want to meet her today or hear anything about her.

'I have to go,' she said, quivering.

'I want you to stay.' He spoke so softly a long burning thrill began to run over her body.

Somehow she had to deny him. Trying to control herself, she clenched her hands together. 'Don't ask this of me, Ben.'

'I'm not asking anything of you but to sit and talk with me a while.'

'I can't. It isn't right.'

'Dani.' He took her resisting hands in his and looked down at her white face, her quivering lips, her green eyes unknowingly glittering with longing. 'We're not doing anything wrong.' He smiled an indulgent smile. A smile that didn't reach his eyes. 'You look so guilty. As if someone's about to come bursting in on us at any minute.'

Crimson washed over her in a great suffocating tide and she felt small and stupid and didn't know why. 'Is that so impossible?'

'Of course it is,' he said easily, very much a man in control. 'This is my home. You don't have to answer to anybody here. And neither do I. Besides, Michael saw me bring you in here. He'll tell the rest of the family if they happen to ask where we are.'

'Doesn't that bother you?' She gave him a long searching look, but the handsome lines in his face told her nothing.

He looked back at her and touched her cheek gently with his finger. 'No. Should it?'

She didn't understand him. Didn't he care what his wife and family thought? It was Christmas and he was throwing a party. He couldn't just walk away from it. If this was how sophisticated people behaved, she wanted no part of it. 'I'm sorry, Ben. I can't stay.'

He turned and walked to the far wall as if he didn't hear her. Pushing a button, a panel slid back to reveal a built-in bar with a shining array of glasses and bottles on lighted glass shelves. 'Surely you won't refuse to have a Christmas drink with me?' He quirked a dark eyebrow at her as she nervously shifted from one foot to the other. 'For old times' sake?'

The breath that was lodged somewhere in the middle of her chest was slowly released in a sigh. She told herself she was acting stupid, reading something into this that wasn't really there. After all, what was so wrong? It was early evening and they were simply two old friends meeting at Christmastime and catching up on old times. She'd forget the uncontrollable way she had thrown herself at him before. That could just be chalked up to six years' worth of pent up emotions. If Libby came looking for him, well, she'd make sure she had nothing to be jealous of.

Accepting the glass he held out to her, with a nervous little lift of her shoulders, she sat back down on the edge of the sofa. Icy shivers ran down her spine and her palms started to sweat and she surrepticiously ran first one then the other over the black material of her dress, looking everywhere but at him.

'Merry Christmas, Dani,' he murmured. His voice was soft, but there was a curious note in it that made her shiver.

She tried not to be so self-conscious. Looking up, she found herself being drawn into the compelling depths of his eyes. He was so very handsome. She saw nothing but that grave and beautiful face with eyes the colour of deep burnished gold shot with sunlight and couldn't look away. But there was something else behind them too, barely hidden, a cold steely quality that confused her.

He reluctantly dragged his eyes away from her and crossed the room to fill another glass, then came back, settling himself easily on the sofa close to her. 'Relax,' he said simply, clinking his glass with hers before taking a deep drink. 'Tell me why you came tonight.'

Swallowing hard and nervously clearing her throat, a red flush rose miserably in her face. How could she pretend he was the same old Ben, interested in what she was doing? He'd gone on while she stayed behind. This beautiful room, the costly furnishings, even the expensive crystal glasses they held in their hands were tangible evidence of the wide gulf between them now.

She did her best to pretend it didn't really matter. 'Oh, I'm a regular Jack of all trades these days—or Jill, to keep the gender right,' she laughed breezily. 'Maurice called the agency I work for needing extra help with this party. And here I am.'

'Agency?'

'Mmm-hmm.' She nodded and pretended to sip her drink. 'Higgins' Domestics on Hay Street.'

He frowned, trying to search her face but she nervously looked away. 'Then it's true? You don't live in Sydney any more? You're not just here visiting for the holidays? You didn't go back after your mother's surgery?' He didn't move, but everything in him seemed to strain closer.

Her heart started fluttering against her ribs and she had trouble breathing as she swirled her drink, watching the liquid move against the sides of the glass. 'No, I'm not visiting. I'm living with my parents again.'

'Why?'

That brought her face back to his with a jerk. He wasn't smiling. His eyes were wintry, the lines at the sides of his mouth hard and set. 'Why shouldn't I?' she asked.

'I thought you loved the bright lights and the fast pace of Sydney?'

'That's not why I went there,' she whispered, a brilliant red rushing to her face. 'You were married and I—I just couldn't stay.'

'Now you're back.' There was steel in his voice. 'Why, Dani? What do you hope to gain?'

'Hope to gain?' She blinked in confusion, not understanding why he sounded so angry. 'I don't hope to gain anything. My mother needed me after her surgery. I decided to stay. It's as simple as that.'

'So simple,' he mocked coldly, his mouth twisting. 'When are you going to start telling me how sick your mother is? How your father's lost his job and is drinking himself into a stupor every night to forget it? How the small amount you bring home and Tom and Renee can spare is what's keeping your family together?'

'That's not true!' she denied hotly, holding herself rigid, refusing to look at him, afraid to see what was in his eyes. 'My mother's not sick. She's doing very well, thank you. And my father goes to work every day. As for his drinking, well, everybody drinks now and then. We're drinking now.' She held up her glass and took a deep reckless swallow then nearly spit it out all over, sucking in a long noisy breath. 'What is this?' she choked, holding her throat.

Ben contained a small smile. 'Brandy,' he said chillingly. 'I knew you were going to need something strong when you started in on the pathos.'

She set the glass on the table and got to her feet looking at him as if he had suddenly developed two heads. He had never used such an ugly tone of voice before, not to her, not ever in all the time she had known him. He was Ben, yet not Ben. The realisation that he really was a complete stranger struck at her and made her quiver with so deep a hurt that she stepped back.

It shouldn't hurt like this, she told herself, mourning the gentle compassionate sensitive man he used to be. It was disappointing, but it wasn't the end of the world. He was nothing to her, after all. And she was nothing to him.

'Thank you for the drink,' she said quietly with a proud lift of her chin. 'I hope you and your family have a nice Christmas.' She turned and started for the door and actually had her hand on the knob when he put a heavy hand on her shoulder, paralyzing her with his touch.

'Surely you're not leaving yet?' he said coldly. 'You haven't got what you came for.'

She swallowed nervously and didn't look at him. 'Which is?'

'Me.'

That brought her around. Violently shrugging off his hand, she looked straight into his sneering face for a full pulsing minute, sixty seconds of stretching, ringing silence.

'Or is it just my money you'll settle for?' he mocked silkily.

Danielle made no attempt to deny it. She continued to keep her eyes on his handsome face now so icy with contempt. Somewhere along the line she had missed something. For some reason he thought she came here tonight with the sole purpose of seeking him out, picking up where they left off and expecting him to pay her for it. But that was absurd. She hadn't even known he lived here. It had come as a shock to her.

Besides, didn't he know if she needed anything, he was the last person she'd ask? She'd go to her father before— The thought stopped dead. That had to be the answer. Her father.

She remembered Ben saying something about her father losing his job and drinking to forget it. How could he know such a thing? Unless— Her mind started to race. Her heart drummed and then everything in her started to collapse.

Oh no, Daddy, you didn't! You didn't lose your job and come to Ben asking for help! Where was your pride?

She was being torn in two. Ice shuddered down her spine and the hair at the back of her neck stood on end. Ben's face swam in and out of focus. She closed her eyes to pull herself together and blink away the sting of unshed tears. Lifting her chin with icy calmness, she looked straight into those chilling gold eyes and said, quite clearly, 'I've changed my mind, Ben. I don't want anything from you after all. Not your money and certainly not you any more. If you'll excuse me?'

He hesitated. Something came and went in his face then he stepped aside, letting her leave him without another word.

CHAPTER FIVE

DANIELLE'S idle gaze wandered past her sister playing on the grass with her children. She wondered if the world would ever stop looking so grey and dreary. Depression had settled on her shoulders like a heavy black cloud. The sun was shining and the wind was hot and blowing through the trees in King's Park with its thousand acres of natural Australian bushland in the heart of the city. It was January in Perth, the middle of summer, but Danielle saw none of it. All she could see for the past three weeks was the unsettling picture of Ben's cold face and grim eyes.

The end of a dream, she told herself for the thousandth time. The end of a dream. The Ben she had known was gone. However much she hated to admit it, he was no longer the man she knew, but he was still the man she loved and that's what galled her. She had to get over him.

Never again would she look into his eyes and see the deep golden glow of innocent enthusiasm. Never again would she see his handsome face crease into a boyish grin, hear his deep velvet voice telling her of his grand plans, feel the strength and protection of his arms in a searingly sweet embrace, taste the gentle passion of his kiss. He was a ruthless stranger, different now, and he hadn't even pretended to be anything else.

She couldn't blame him for his reaction to seeing her on Christmas Eve. When she finally got home that night and confronted her father, it all came spilling out and then she understood so many things.

'Oh, Dad,' she said, 'how could you?'

He tried to bluff his way out of it but the amount of alcohol he had consumed all that day loosened his tongue and he told her everything. Her mother had gone to bed and they sat at the kitchen table with his ever present bottle of whisky in front of him. 'I lost my job, Dani. I couldn't let your mother know about it, not with Christmas and all. She needs to be protected. I still don't know how I'm going to tell her. It was easier to pretend to go to work every day.'

She bit her lip. 'How long have you been pretending?'

'Six weeks,' he said guiltily.

'Oh Dad! Where do you go instead?' She stirred sugar into her coffee and weakly subsided back in the chair across from him.

'I sit in the park and watch the boats go by.'

'All day?' she gasped.

He coloured slightly. 'Well, no. Sometimes I stop for a drop or two at the pub round the corner.'

'Oh Dad!' There was no censure in her voice, only despair. 'What made you go to Ben to ask for money?'

'You told me how successful he was, remember? I thought he would understand. I went to him on the first of December and told him we were destitute except for what you brought home. It wasn't so long ago since he was that way himself that he would forget.' He took a long indignant swallow of whiskey and wiped his mouth with the back of his hand. 'But I didn't come right out and ask him for money, so don't get upset. I still have some pride, you know. I didn't expect a handout. I asked him for a job.'

'But why Ben?'

'Who better?' he shot back. 'He's a very influential man these days. And he loved you once. And you still love him. You told me so.'

Her face flamed. 'What did he say?'

'He asked me a lot of questions. Mostly about you. Did you know he thought you were married? He said something about you wearing a wedding ring when he saw you at the hospital when your mother had surgery. I think he was relieved when he found out you weren't.'

'Oh Dad!'

'Will you stop "Oh Dad-ing" me?' he said irritably, taking another long swallow of whisky. He looked at her then quickly looked away. His eyes were bloodshot and his hands shook. 'He still loves you, Dani. I could tell. You were his first love and he's never forgotten what you meant to him.'

'Oh Da——' She put her hand to her mouth to bite back the words. This was so much worse than she thought. How could her father try to take advantage of something so long dead? She looked at him with bleak bitterness. 'Don't you see? That was in the past. We're both different people now. You were wrong to try to trade on that. I hope he told you no.'

He drew back in surprise, never taking his eyes off her pale set face. 'He said yes. I'm to start working for him after the first of the year.'

She let out a small breath. 'I see.'

'No you don't.' He rested his palms flat on the table and looked at them for a long time in silence. When he looked up again there was a certain implacability about his mouth.

'He's given me a job in the North West Shelf Gas Fields,' he said, trying not to slur his words. 'I have to talk your mother into moving north with me when I go.'

She closed her eyes and uttered an agonized sound. 'You know she won't do that. She always said she wouldn't be happy anywhere else but here.'

'Then the whole thing's off. That was one of his conditions. If she doesn't come with me, I don't have a job. And that means I'll have to find some way to pay back the advance he gave me.'

'Advance?' Her eyes widened.

'Five thousand dollars,' he said defensively. 'I need something for us to live on until the first of the year. And I'll have to find a place to live when we get up north. And there were all those Christmas gifts I wanted you children to have . . .'

Danielle didn't move. The bleakness in her eyes hardened. 'That's just one of the conditions? Are there others?'

He took another nervous drink and started to weave back and forth in his chair. 'I don't know how to tell you.'

There was a sudden hard silence in the room and a shiver of fear ran through her.

'He wants you,' he finally whispered hoarsely, 'to go to him and ask for his help.'

She stared at him in horror then jumped to her feet, trembling violently.

'And then you're to tell him how grateful we are,' he said with deadly calm.

'*No!*' He wouldn't trample on her pride like that. Not Ben. 'He couldn't!'

He had shrugged as if her pride was inconsequential and she had seen clearly for the first time, her father's self-centeredness, his weakness and compliance and yielding to those stronger than he. His tie was loose about his neck, his white shirt creased and wrinkled. His bushy white hair stood on end where he had been running his hands through it. His face was congested and lined and mottled. He was quite drunk.

Letting out her breath, she took her cup and poured the coffee down the sink, every movement measured and calm, but inside she was seething with anger and confusion. Her thoughts were turbulent, chaotic, sick with pain and shaking with denial. 'How could Ben ask such a thing?' she whispered through stiff lips. 'And how could you agree to it? Don't you realise how demeaning that would be for me? Mum always said he wasn't good enough for me. Now to have me go to him and ask for help . . .'

'There was nothing else I could do. He was my last hope.'

'Oh, Dad,' she said bitterly, turning to face him. Her mouth twisted. 'No wonder he acted so strange tonight. He actually thought I was there because you sent me!'

He blinked his bleary eyes and tried to focus on her. 'What do you mean?'

A small sick laugh escaped her. 'The party I worked tonight was Ben's.'

He hiccupped loudly and swayed, getting to his feet. 'You saw him then?' He had trouble keeping her in focus. 'You didn't do anything to spoil things for me, did you?'

'Oh no,' she said resentfully, 'nothing's spoiled for you. But do you know how I feel? Ben actually thought . . . ' Her voice trailed away with utter humiliation and a long slow shivering passed over her body. Ben thought she had come to him to beg.

Why? She asked herself that question a thousand times since that night. What did Ben get out of it?

As the long miserable holidays passed, she did a lot of hard thinking and finally came up with the only answer that made any sense. Revenge. She had hurt him all those years ago and this was his way of getting his own back, of having her acknowledge what she missed. But it was such a small victory. And so unworthy of him. Disappointment swamped her. It was a hard thing to admit that Ben had his faults just like everybody else. She had put him on a pedestal for so long and thought him so far above such a petty thing. It was disillusioning to find he was human after all.

'Dani? Did you hear me?'

Startled, Danielle looked up to see her sister standing in front of her. Her thoughts were so vivid and had taken her so far that she was surprised to find herself in the park with Renee. 'Sorry,' she blinked. 'I guess I was daydreaming. What did you say?'

Renee sighed, plopping down beside her on the park bench and wiping her hand across her eyes. 'It doesn't really matter. Want to tell me about him?'

'Him? Who?'

'"Who?" she asks. It's got to be a man to make you block out everything going on around you on a beautiful day like this. Come on, tell me who's finally taken Ben Harper's place.'

Danielle swallowed back the pain his name brought on. 'I was thinking about Daddy, actually.'

Renee lifted her shapely leg in white shorts. 'Go ahead. Pull the other one.'

'No, really. I was wondering how he managed to talk Mum into going north with him. She would never so much as take a holiday before, let alone sell the house and move!'

'You mean you honestly don't know?'

'Do you? All Daddy would tell me was it took some doing, but he finally got her to agree.'

'They're getting on in years, you know. It was time for them to make the move. We're all grown and independent now. Besides, you underestimate the power of money,' Renee said cynically, shaking her head. 'Once he told her the salary involved, do you honestly think she would stand in his way?'

'It was very generous, wasn't it?' Danielle said in a small voice, frowning, wondering again how Ben could be so generous to her father if he wanted his revenge so much.

'The thing I can't figure out is how Daddy managed to find such a position at his age— and just when he needed it too,' Renee mused, watching her boys feeding the black swans in the water a short distance away.

If her father didn't tell her about Ben's part in it, Danielle wasn't going to. 'A stroke of luck, pure and simple.'

'Mmm-hmm.' Renee didn't sound convinced. 'And what about him coming up with enough money to get you enrolled in art school as a Christmas present? Are you going to tell me that was luck too?'

Danielle gritted her teeth. 'What else could it be?'

'I don't know. But you do. And that's why you're refusing to start classes. It's what you always wanted, but now that it's been handed to you, you're passing it up.'

'Let it go, Renee.'

'No. I won't let it go. There's something going on here that you're not telling me and I'll bet it's got something to do with Ben Harper.'

Danielle laughed a little wildly. 'You always did have a vivid imagination. Ben Harper has nothing to do with anything.'

'Ben Harper has everything to do with you. You're so solitary these days, refusing even the most casual date. If you've really let him go like you said you have, you wouldn't still be comparing every man you meet to Ben and finding him wanting.'

Expelling her breath, she shook her head with grudging affection. Renee meant well, she supposed, but Danielle couldn't help wishing she would stop treating her as if she was incapable of handling her own life. She had moved in with her temporarily, until she could afford a place of her own, but Renee was becoming more and more overbearing without realising it.

Renee's face flushed with sudden triumph

when she saw Danielle squirming guiltily.
'I'm right, aren't I? You're still all tied up
with Ben. Why, I wouldn't be surprised if he
didn't give Daddy the money——' she
stopped and her eyes suddenly widened and
her mouth fell open. 'Good Lord,' she
whispered, 'that's it, isn't it? Ben gave Daddy
the money—and the job.'

Danielle looked at her with a feeling of
despair. 'Yes,' she said quietly, her voice
underlining every word, 'after Daddy went to
him and asked.'

Renee was speechless.

'So now you know.' She stood up. 'That's
why I'm so angry and why I can't go to art
school. Ben's paying for it!' She looked at her
with all the barely contained fury of her
stubborn nature and after a moment she
walked away, shaking horribly, blinking back
the sharp sting of tears.

Renee sought her out after a while. She had
packed up her children and was ready to go
home, but Danielle didn't want to leave yet.
Long after Renee had gone, she stayed in the
park sitting on a secluded bench watching the
sun slowly sink into the water. A lonely peace
settled over everything and she tried to
absorb some of it, but her mind was too
restless to relax. Lights began to twinkle in
some of the office buildings across the river

and she found herself wondering if one of them was Ben's and if he was still at work or if he had gone home already.

The breeze was cooler now and gentle. She couldn't help remembering how she and Ben used to walk here hand in hand, enjoying what he called the 'Fremantle Doctor'. In late afternoon and early evening, the hot summer air would change when the sea breeze came up the Swan River from the Indian Ocean port of Fremantle . . .

She stopped herself at once and shook her head. Why was it every thought she had, sooner or later returned to Ben? She had to put him behind her. He had changed. He was gone. She didn't love him any more. She wouldn't love him.

'Dani?' His gentle voice sounded so real behind her she jerked violently. 'I thought it was you. In all the times I've come here, I've never run into you before.'

Oh, great, she thought, now she was hallucinating. She swallowed hard and turned, not really expecting to see him here. This had to be her imagination. He was probably at home right now eating dinner with his wife and a few of his wealthy friends. She could almost hear the soft whisper of his servants' feet, the gentle murmur of refined conversation, the muted chink of silver against bone china plates.

But there he stood, all alone behind her, tall and handsome, his white shirt open at his throat, his tie loosened, his grey jacket slung over one shoulder. He was smiling, his teeth a bright white slash against his tan. There was no mistaking it was Ben. No one else had that lean indolent grace or that silky black hair that persisted in falling over his forehead. No one else held such magnetism for her. Even now she could feel every inch of her skin tingling with yearning just from looking at him.

Hating the idea that she could let him affect her this way, she ground her teeth together and started to get to her feet. 'I was just leaving,' she whispered.

His hand descended on her shoulder. 'Don't go.'

She glanced anxiously about her. They were all alone in the deepening dusk with nothing but the birds settling in the trees and the black swans on the river and the wild flowers gently moving in the fragrant grass.

'You're afraid of me, Dani, and I never wanted that.' His deep voice was husky and he sounded wounded.

She looked him full in the face, following his movements with a helpless attention to detail as he sat down and forced her to sit beside him. She didn't want to notice how tired and dispirited he looked, but she couldn't help it. His eyes were positively haunted. For some reason he was deeply troubled and he looked vulnerable and that surprised her. She had always thought of him as strong. Nothing could touch Ben that he didn't want to touch him. He was a man always in control

'I'm not afraid of you,' she said shakily, her lashes flickering, before she dragged her eyes away and bent her head.

It was torture sitting here beside him, not touching, but oh, so aware of him. Aware and *wanting*. She flayed herself inwardly. He had demeaned her. How could she lose all her resolve to stay cool and aloof and detached the minute she saw him again? He was not the Ben she knew, she reminded herself. He was vengeful. He manipulated people for some perverse satisfaction of his own. Hadn't he forced her parents to move north? Hadn't he forced her out of her home and into Renee's? Forced her to give up her dream of attending art school? He had to know she would never attend once she realised he was paying for it.

'Dani,' he repeated slowly. And when she looked up at him he lifted his hand, unable to resist the temptation to trail the back of it down her cheek.

'Please——' she breathed sharply, turning her head away.

'You do,' he said softly, '. . . please me.'

When she turned back helplessly, his mouth came down on hers. Not hard, not punishing or aggressive, just in a series of light, compelling kisses that dissolved all her pent up tension and made her respond to him unthinkingly. He was Ben, her Ben, sweeping her back into the past.

Yielding, pliant, it was the most natural thing in the world for her to open her mouth to the sweet remembered invasion of his. It brought a sense of homecoming. Everything was right again. He hadn't stopped being gentle or masterful. His hands cradled her face, holding her captive, tantalising her, making the warm rush of desire burst and flower in her.

Her body was straining toward his now, her senses beginning to swim with rising frustration. He seemed content to play with her mouth, his lips softly moving on hers, his tongue gently teasing. She could feel the heat of his thigh barely brushing against hers, but he didn't seem to want to make closer contact and with a helpless little whimper she lifted her hands and gripped his shoulders, pressing herself into him, fusing her mouth to his.

His control deserted him. Demanding now,

and hungry and passionate, he wound his strong arms around her, almost crushing her slender body, shuddering as desire ran between them like a raging fire.

Her hands were in his hair, twining, clinging, stroking the silky black thickness. Her fingers traced the sensitive skin at the back of his neck and behind his ears and travelled the long length of his back, delighting in every hard bone and clenching muscle. The heavy throbbing of his heart and the pulsing heat of his body made her fiercely aware of his arousal.

Her whole body seemed to vibrate in reaction. She was alive and rapturous and exultant.

Ben was breathing hard. Beads of moisture sprang out on his skin. 'Dani, Dani, I want you,' he murmured brokenly, his lips moving down the long warm curve of her neck. 'I've never stopped wanting you. I thought I'd have my revenge, but it wasn't what I wanted. I want you!'

Danielle flung her head back, her face radiant, her hair tumbling down her back in a dark brown wave. The buttons of her blouse had come undone and her breasts spilled into his hands, soft and white and swollen. The blood was singing in her ears and her heart melted and flowed out to him on an irresistible tide of desire. She wanted to give him all that was hers to give. She loved him more than it was possible to love a man. Forgotten was the insult to her pride and self-respect. She no longer thought of him as a married man who had been hurt and wanted his revenge. Everything that had gone before was irrelevant. His hands and mouth were everywhere, making her forget everything.

The darkness deepened all around them. There were only the two of them, alone in the deserted park with the soft scented nighttime sharpening their senses. The breeze was cool and fresh. A dreamlike haze settled on the river with its murmuring mouth gently lapping the grassy banks. Even as the translucent water was moving, so were her hands, restless and hungry for the feel of him. It made her dizzy and for a moment she wondered when she had unbuttoned his shirt, but then it didn't matter. All she knew was he was letting her touch him too, letting her glory in the feel of all his warm moist skin. Her fingers slid and bumped across the wide expanse of his chest, curled into his taut muscles, flattened on the hardened tips of his nipples. When she put her lips to them a groan came from somewhere deep inside him. She felt his passion and his gentleness and then his sudden loss of control. It was this last that brought her back to her senses with a shuddering pang of regret. She didn't have the right to love him like this. Stiffening in his arms, she held her hands away from his chest and looked straight into his eyes.

The bright burnished gold was ringed with dark desire and she had to fight this boneless yearning to silence her conscience and listen only to her heart. Ben's handsome features had changed, become lost and open and vulnerable. She couldn't drag her eyes away from him. The wind rose, and the voice of the river, but everything else was silent, hushed, waiting.

Then a shattering realisation hit her. She had the power to hurt him. He was handing her that power now, letting her do what she would do. Her heart swelled one moment and in the next was squeezed with anguish. Her whole body became cold and she shivered with a strange desolation. She had hurt him once before, all those years ago. She wouldn't do it again. She wanted to cry out to him to go away and leave her alone. If she stayed here and gave in to this forbidden desire, she would end up hurting him more than before. She would become his mistress and when this passion waned, he would hate her for allowing him to betray his wife.

Her breathing was nothing more than long ragged gasps in the ringing silence. Her lips were numb, her eyes stinging. Somehow she broke away from him and dragged the sides of her blouse together, fumbling with the buttons, lifting her chin much too high.

'I'm sorry, Ben,' she said softly, a faint grimness stealing into her husky voice. 'I can't.'

'You can't ... what?' he said shakily, not moving.

'I don't know why you came here or what you want of me. Whatever it is, I can't do it.'

Ben said nothing. Even in the darkness he was caught and held by the strange glittering green of her eyes and the hard sadness of her glowing mouth. She had never looked more beautiful to him, sitting here bristling with uneasy indignation. Her legs were long and slender and shapely in her white shorts. Her simple pink blouse made her pale skin glow. Her long hair tumbled on her shoulders with a vital glowing darkness. He made a sudden movement towards her and then just as suddenly stopped, his hand hovering near the side of her head as if he wanted to touch her, but dared not.

'We have to finish what we started all those years ago,' he said quietly.

Her throat closed and her mouth became as

dry as death. She tried to swallow but couldn't, tried to speak but no sound came. Hot bitter tears stood in her eyes. A deep wash of colour ran up her neck and her whole body vibrated with yearning. What she wouldn't give to be able to go back and wipe away the hurt of the past, start over again, love him like he had never been loved before. But it was impossible. She knew it. There was too much between them now. Too much hurt and mistrust and past injustice. There was no way to make it right. And besides, there was his wife.

'You want to finish what we started?' she heard herself ask in a cold hard voice that shook and wobbled in spite of herself. She couldn't let him pretend his wife didn't matter. 'What does Libby have to say about this?'

Ben's head went back as if she had struck him. He stared hard at her then dropped his hand and stiffened, turning very white beneath his tan. He sat in silence, his eyes fixed on her face before muttering in a shattered, angry voice, 'She's dead, Dani. Don't you know that? Do you think I'd be sitting here with you, saying these things to you now, if she wasn't?'

CHAPTER SIX

THE loathing in his voice drove all the colour from her face. Stunned, she could only look at him with wide, stricken eyes. So many things swirled through her mind, shame and embarrassment and anger even while inexplicable pain clawed at her. 'That's exactly what I thought,' she whispered.

Something snapped inside him. His eyes closed. His fists involuntarily doubled. Then all his expression vanished as he fought for control. His lips shook when he turned, almost woodenly, away from her.

'I'm sorry, Ben,' she broke in breathlessly. She should have realised such brutal honesty would only hurt him. 'I ... didn't know about Libby.'

'No?' His jaw clenched and his dark brows rose as he turned back to her. 'It was in all the papers.'

His patent disbelief made something twist inside her. 'I don't make a habit of reading the society pages!' she flared, then was instantly ashamed when she heard his quick wounded gasp. That was unthinkingly cruel and he didn't deserve that, no matter what a beating her pride had to take. She backed down at once. 'I'm sorry. That was uncalled for. I don't know why I said that.' Impulsively, she put her hand on his arm and flinched at his automatic recoil, but the question spilled from her lips anyway, 'What happened? Had she been sick? Was it an accident?'

Something came and went in his eyes, almost a kind of hope, then they narrowed as he searched her face for a long moment. 'You really don't know, do you?'

She looked uncertain.

'She died the same night Christopher was born.'

'Christopher?'

'My son,' he said flatly.

Her mouth started to fall open, but she quickly snapped it shut. 'But I was with you that night. At the hospital. That's when my mother had surgery. The doctor came and told you she was all right!'

Ben said nothing. He looked at her with a strange miserable expression full of bleakness and wretchedness and anguish. 'I thought that too, at the time, but you know how doctors are. They never come right out and tell you anything. If you remember, all he really said was it was touch and go for a while, but she never gave up. And then he said she was asking for me.' Deep blue lines sprang out at the sides of his mouth. 'He was losing her but he didn't tell me. She tried to hang on but she died before I got to her.' He uttered an agonised sound and turned away, helplessly burying his face in his hands.

Danielle sucked in a harsh rasping breath, too stunned to say a word.

Almost huddling on the bench beside her in the darkness, Ben began to mutter brokenly, 'My wife was dying, but I was with you. I remember holding your hand.' His ragged voice was barely audible now, the words harsh and disjointed. 'That wedding ring on your finger. Shiny gold. All I could think of, all I could picture, you . . . married . . . some other man. You loved someone else. Not me.' He slowly lifted his face then and the moonlight struck full on his rigid features. Tears stood in his eyes. 'My wife was dying, but all I could see was you!'

Their eyes locked, stricken gold and glittering green, and then she knew.

He loved her once and now he hated her. Somehow in his anguished mind he blamed her for his wife's death.

Ice shuddered down Danielle's spine. Her skin prickled and a sick feeling clutched at her stomach. Her throat throbbed and she struggled to swallow, her chest hurting with the effort to breathe. Somehow she managed to find a restrained, if halting, voice. 'You make it sound as if we planned to meet there, Ben.'

'Planned?'

She could tell the thought was new to him. He blinked, rubbing trembling hands over his face before falling into a desperate silence, clenching and unclenching his fists.

His perspective was all wrong. She had to make him see that he hadn't betrayed his wife by waiting with her. 'It was accidental,' she said quietly after a long moment. 'We simply happened to be in the same place at the same time, that's all. I was waiting for my mother. You were waiting for Libby. You were the last person I expected to see that day.'

He lifted his head. For a moment wild hope flashed in his eyes, but it was quickly doused. She knew he wanted to believe her, but this irrational guilt was too much a part of him.

'You have nothing to berate yourself for,' she said in a practical voice without emotion. 'And there's no reason to hate me. We did nothing wrong.'

'We did,' he countered bitterly. 'I did. I should have been with Libby.'

'You would have been if it weren't for hospital rules.'

He faltered, drawing a deep breath as if he felt smothered. 'She needed me and I wasn't there.'

'You were as near as they allowed you to be.'

'I failed her.'

'You failed no one. You were there. And she knew you were there.'

'She was alone!' He looked straight at her and again a look of loathing and disgust flared on his face. 'I was with *you*.'

Silence stretched between them then Danielle straightened her shoulders, her eyes glittering. 'Oh no, Ben. I'm not accepting the blame for this.' The moonlight lay in the sockets of her eyes and shone on the stoniness of her mouth. 'I've done a lot of things wrong where you're concerned, but not this. I sat with you that night because I thought you needed someone. I was glad to be there especially after everything I did before to hurt you. I thought I was making up for it. I was helping you in some way. I didn't know you would twist it until it became just another reason to despise me. If I had it to do over again, I would do it.' She raised her head proudly and became very still. 'Just remember this, Ben,' her voice was quiet and intense, 'I took nothing away from Libby when I sat with you!'

He stared at her and Danielle had to wonder if he really even saw her. He was so swallowed up in his own abysmal guilt and grief. Something must have reached him though, because his bowed shoulders straightened and the slack hands on his knees tightened.

'Why didn't you go north with your parents?' he asked hoarsely.

She hesitated, not following his train of thought. 'Is that what you expected me to do?'

'Yes. I didn't expect you to stay here and move in with Renee.'

She took a deep calming breath. 'Well, I'm sorry to disappoint you, but you were wrong to think you could manipulate me.'

'I wasn't manipulating anybody.'

'Of course you were,' she said tightly, not even trying to tone down the bitterness in her voice. 'You were getting even with me for leaving you six years ago. You knew I was alone except for them so you banished my mother and father——'

'Banished?' he broke in roughly. 'I gave your father a job.'

'You sent them away under the guise of a job.'

'I was trying to help him.'

'In return for my abject gratitude.' Her lip

curled. 'And just how did you expect me to show you that gratitude, Ben? Or shall I guess?'

His face darkened. 'You've got it all wrong.'

'Have I? Have I really?' Icy fury began welling up in her and she barely managed to contain it. 'Wasn't that one of your conditions? That I come and tell you how grateful I am? That I acknowledge the great Ben Harper deciding to be magnanimous? Stooping to help the girl who once thought he wasn't good enough?'

His whole body jerked violently as if she had struck him.

She stopped dead, staring at him, her colour flooding away. The words rang out shockingly clear in the cool night air, spreading like ripples in a pond, before she swallowed convulsively to keep back a sob. And then the only sound was her breathing, loud and swift and shallow.

'So that's why,' he whispered, slowly lifting his head and pinning her with flaring gold eyes. 'I wondered if you would ever find the courage to tell me.'

Danielle wanted to deny it, to shift the blame, to tell him it was all her mother's doing. She hadn't really felt he wasn't good enough for her. She had been so young and impressionable then. But she knew she would be stupid to keep trying to hide the truth from herself. Her mother might have pointed out Ben's unsuitability, but in the end it was her own choice to tell him goodbye.

Suddenly, without warning, she couldn't control the tears choking her throat. She made no effort to turn away, nor did she make a sound. The tears simply ran from her eyes and fell down her white face in an acid flood. She remembered Ben saying earlier that they had to finish what they started six years ago. Well, she had no doubt she had finished it now.

She could see the past with a newfound clarity and it made her ashamed. Too much a coward before, she hadn't let herself see it, preferring instead to blame her mother. But now she looked and she saw. Everything had changed. Never again could she think herself the innocent, wronged by circumstances and an overbearing mother. She had hurt him all by herself and it was time to accept the responsibility for it. In the end the choice had been hers. Deep down she must have thought he wasn't good enough or she wouldn't have done it.

And then too, there was the way she had left him. She never told him why. She let him think she simply lost interest, that their love had run its course, burned itself out. She knew he loved her. In that way she was subconsciously leaving the door open so one day he would come back. She hadn't had the decency to set him free.

She was appalled to think how she must have come between him and his wife all this time, but she forced herself to think about it now and see how unfair she had been. No matter what he did or where he went, she made sure she stayed in the back of his mind like a loose end, not wanting him, but not letting him go either.

And all because he wasn't good enough, because at the time he had no prospects for a wealthy future. She closed her eyes and mentally flayed herself. The irony of their vastly changed circumstances now was not lost on her.

Oh, Ben, she thought with aching regret. How could she have done that to him? How could she have tried to destroy this man who was worth ten of anybody else?

At last, feeling bruised and aching in every muscle, she stood on trembling legs and straightened, facing him in the shimmering moonlight. Wiping her tears away with the backs of her hands, she made herself stand still. Her voice shook. She cleared her throat and faltered, struggling to make it loud enough for him to hear. 'I'm sorry, Ben. I know it doesn't help you to hear that now but I truly am sorry. If I could go back, if I could do things differently ...' She gave an unsteady laugh. 'But I know that's impossible. Maybe someday you can find it in your heart to forgive me. I wouldn't blame you if you never did. But maybe someday you will.'

There was a long silence. She knew he was looking at her. She could feel his eyes touching her. But she didn't know if he understood what she was saying. The moonlight distorted his expression and she had to wonder if she was imagining the bitter pain running across his face. A muscle jerked and quivered in his cheek. His chest rose and fell. The breeze lifted his hair and blew it across his forehead. Then almost as if he couldn't stand to look at her any longer, he stiffly averted his head, turning away in silent repudiation.

Her heart plunged. She knew. It was over. The knowledge settled in her chest like a cold hard lump. He didn't have to say a word. The stiff way he held himself spoke volumes.

Somehow she made herself turn. One leaden foot blindly followed the other across the uneven grass, past the gently lapping water, beside the fragrant flower beds. The darkness swallowed her up as she picked her way out of the park alone.

When Ben turned back, she was gone.

For many weeks after that Danielle felt she was poised at the edge of a steep cliff just waiting for one false move to tumble her headlong into oblivion. She tried not to think of Ben. She didn't hear from him. And then she had to wonder if she really expected to. She couldn't forget the look on his face, or his stillness, or her own anguish. But it was done and day after day she told herself she had to go on in spite of it. Finally as summer turned into autumn she began to accept it and forgive herself a little and get on with her life. She had wronged a gentle man and there was nothing she could do about it now. It's over, she kept telling herself. It's over.

Renee wasn't aware of what had happened. She only knew something was wrong. 'You're getting so thin,' she said to Danielle one brisk May evening after dinner. The air was crisp, filled with the scent of woodsmoke from neighbouring cottages, and Jack had taken the boys out for a walk while they did the dishes. 'How do you expect to keep up this murderous pace?'

'What murderous pace?' Danielle answered, putting down the dish towel and bracing herself against her sister's searching look.

A very soft, very eloquent sigh sounded in Renee's throat. She stood with her soapy hands on her hips looking very much like their mother without meaning to. 'Danielle, Jack told me to mind my own business, but I feel responsible for you. You're your own person and you don't have to answer to me just because you live here with us but I saw the way you were when you went with us to visit Mum and Dad. Twice now you've spent the entire time cleaning house for them instead of relaxing. It was supposed to be a holiday! And you work the most ungodly hours for that blasted agency. And you never turn down any job, no matter how unsuitable it is. And lately I've noticed the light burning in your room long after everyone else has gone to bed. Good grief, aren't you afraid you're going to drop in your tracks?'

'It's not as bad as all that,' she said with a small bright smile that didn't fool Renee for a minute. 'Mum and Dad were grateful for the help. They're getting on in years, you know. And Miss Higgins knows I'm reliable. That's why she recommends me for so many jobs. I don't like to let people down, so I take them. And I'm trying to paint at night so I don't lose what I've learned so far. I'm sorry if I'm bothering you.'

'You're not bothering me and you know it.

I think I know why you're keeping yourself so busy, but it's no good. Mum's the one who put the bug in my ear about you looking so peaky. Even Daddy could see the change in you now that he's stopped drinking.'

Danielle seized on that in an effort to sidetrack her. Her voice softened. 'Who would have thought he was on his way to be rehabilitated in an alcoholic programme when he left here?' she murmured. 'That job was just an excuse to get him to go north. The new surroundings, new people, even the foreman who took him under his wing, all helped him to stop drinking.'

Not really diverted, Renee shook her head and sighed. 'It's strange how that worked out, isn't it? All of a sudden Daddy found it easy to give up that crutch and take control of his life again.' Then her smile became rueful. 'But maybe it's not so strange, knowing Ben was at the bottom of it. He must still care for you or else he wouldn't have done that. Mum said she'd always be indebted to him.'

Danielle's mouth twisted at the irony. 'My, my, how things have changed.' Sarcasm dripped from her. 'Once he wasn't good enough. Now she's indebted to him.'

'You aren't,' Renee said, her voice oddly hesitant. 'What's stopping you from going back to him now that you told me he's a widower?'

Danielle's eyes widened. 'How can I go back? Once I thought he wasn't good enough. Now that he's wealthy, how would he be sure that's not the attraction? He would never believe I wanted him for himself not for his money.'

Renee shifted uncomfortably. 'You love him. And he loves you. It's always been that way between you. Nothing's changed.'

'Everything's changed. Can you honestly see me going up to him and saying, "Forget everything that happened in the past, Ben. I'm here now and I'm yours if you'd care to have me"?' Her mouth shook and she began to laugh, but it sounded more like a sob. 'I hurt him too deeply. He doesn't want me now. There's no way I can make things up to him. Besides, he can have his pick of any woman in the world. There's not a thing I can give him that he couldn't get better somewhere else.'

'Danielle! You've got a lot to offer any man if only you'd see it.' She made a sound of exasperation then turned back to the sink and took out her frustration on a frying pan. 'You should realise Ben couldn't have done what he did for Daddy if he didn't still have some feeling for you. He made our problems his because he cares. Why don't you go to him and talk it all out?'

'I can't. He doesn't want to see me. Believe me, he doesn't want to see me.' She pictured again the stiff turn of his head and his silent repudiation, and her heart squeezed painfully.

CHAPTER SEVEN

NOTHING was going right for her any more, Danielle thought. All throwing herself into a frenetic whirl of constantly changing jobs with new faces and varied scenery had done, was to undermine her physical stamina. Ben's face ran through her mind a thousand times a day and her nights were long and restless and punctuated with impossible dreams. She thought of leaving Perth, of going back to Sydney again, but she knew the width of the continent between them wouldn't help at all. He lived in her heart and no matter where she went, she took him with her.

She was sweeping the floor in a busy little restaurant near Hyde Park at the beginning of December when a man came in right at closing time and sat down at one of the small tables. In his mid-sixties, he was dressed in a lightweight grey suit. Clean shaven, his hair was pure white and he had a tanned weathered face and bright blue eyes that twinkled up at her.

'I'm sorry, sir, we are just about to close,' she said gently, forcibly sending an unbidden thought of Ben scurrying out of her mind.

He slid the colourful menu back on the table between the salt shaker and the sugar bowl and gave her a grave smile. 'Will there be time for a cup of tea?'

She hesitated only a moment then smiled back at him before putting her broom down. 'Of course.'

When she set a steaming cup in front of him he nodded his thanks and let his eyes wander around the nearly empty restaurant. Two people were finishing a last cup of coffee and a truck driver had just walked to the woman behind the cash register to pay for his meal. 'Will you join me?' he asked.

She didn't want to. It had been a long day and she was looking forward to going home and soaking her feet before once again trying to tackle the portrait she had been fighting all week. Landscapes came easy to her, but portraits were proving to be her weak point. But the man's eyes twinkled so engagingly she found herself agreeing in spite of herself. She would be late getting home, but putting off painting one more night wouldn't hurt anything.

'I'm Rupert Jones,' he said, holding out his hand when she seated herself across the table from him with her own cup.

His handshake was surprisingly warm, considering he was a stranger to her.

'How do you do? I'm Danielle Williams.'

'I know.'

She blinked.

'Agatha Higgins described you in perfect detail and told me where to find you.' He studied her face with its fair skin and tired green eyes. Her hair was pulled on top of her head and twisted into a knot, but long brown wisps had managed to escape down the back of her neck and around her ears to soften the plainness of her features. He smiled gently.

'You were looking for me?' she frowned.

'You could say that, yes.' He lightly curled one hand around his cup while the other slowly circled the rim.

He had nice hands, Danielle thought inconsequentially. Then she found herself comparing them to Ben's. Ben had long fingers too, with the nails clipped short like these. They were strong and tanned and full of power, yet they could be so amazingly gentle. She remembered how she felt when Ben used to hold her, those supple fingers stroking her skin . . .

She almost shuddered and dragged her eyes away from Rupert Jones' hands back to his face.

A faint smile lifted the corners of his mouth as if he knew what she was thinking and, oddly, his eyes crinkled as he nodded with gentle understanding.

'Do I know you?' she asked, taking a deep breath and trying not to be disconcerted by his attitude of amused indulgence. He was a stranger. She was sure of it.

'We've never met.'

'That's odd. I feel as if we have.'

His smile deepened. 'I've been told that on a number of occasions.' He took a sip of his tea and made an appreciative murmur. 'I came to ask a favour of you, Miss Williams.'

'Please call me Dani,' she smiled, liking this man at once and feeling strangely at ease with him. He was a comfortable person and she inexplicably felt she had known him all her life. 'I'll be glad to help you in any way I can.'

'Dani,' he nodded again, 'I need you to come and be my housekeeper. Agatha Higgins says you're just the girl I'm looking for.'

Flattered by the compliment, Danielle laughed a little self-consciously. This wasn't the usual way she met her prospective employers, but then he was an unusual man. 'Very well,' she agreed. 'If Miss Higgins thinks so, I won't argue with that. I presume she's told you the girl I'm replacing here won't be back for another week, but after that I'll be free to work for you?'

His eyes twinkled. 'She told me. There's

one thing I must ask, though. This is more in the nature of a permanent job. Will you consent to live in?'

'Oh,' she said softly.

'I understand you do temporary work, but Miss Higgins told me you've been thinking of changing that? Your parents recently moved, and you've been living with your sister until you can find a place of your own, is that right?'

She nodded, wondering why Miss Higgins had volunteered such information without checking with her first. But then she thought that was hardly surprising. He was a man who invited confidences. His voice was gentle, his face so very kind. She again thought it strange that she should feel so at ease with him. Usually she was timid and shy around strangers.

'Perhaps this will suit both of us,' he said quietly. 'You need a place to live. I need someone to care for my home. I used to have a daughter about your age.' His eyes took on a faraway look. 'She died a little more than a year ago. First my wife, then my daughter. Since that time I've been letting things slide.' He closed his eyes a minute, then blinked them open again and smiled brightly. 'My son-in-law finally convinced me it was time to stop grieving, time to go on living. So . . .' He spread his hands. 'Will you help me?'

Danielle's shoulders lifted in wordless sympathy. 'I'm so sorry, Mr Jones. It must be lonely for you. What would you have me do?'

'Thank you, my dear. As for your duties, they would be the usual; cleaning, laundry, grocery shopping, preparing light meals. I live very simply and I don't demand perfection.'

She hesitated. For some reason she was afraid she would disappoint him.

'The salary Miss Higgins suggested seemed a bit low,' he said quietly, his eyes full of gentle understanding. 'Would you consider this?'

The figure he named made her swallow hard. It had to be too good to be true. Only yesterday she and Miss Higgins were discussing whether a permanent job might be what she needed to give her a sense of stability. Now to have this gentle man come and offer her just what she was looking for and with such a generous salary and without seeming to expect too much, made her wary. Apprehension shimmered darkly green in the depths of her eyes.

He smiled. 'It's not really too good to be true, you know. I can be a bear at times, especially after a hard day at work.'

A small laugh escaped her. 'Is mind reading one of your attributes as well?'

'No, my dear. You simply have a very expressive face. I'd like to paint you one day, if I may?'

Her mouth fell open and she leaned a little closer to him. 'Paint? You mean like in portrait painting?'

He nodded, frowning a little at her apparent surprise. 'I'm semi-retired, but I teach a class three days a week at the University. Don't tell me you're an artist?'

'It's a fading dream of mine,' she said breathlessly.

'Ah.' There was a wealth of satisfaction in the word. 'Perhaps you'll let me help you rekindle the dream?'

Now Danielle's head really spun. There had to be a catch somewhere. Things like this just didn't happen to people like her. It was all a little too pat. Just like that job of her father's. But Ben had been behind that one, sending him north to be rehabilitated without letting any of them know that was the real reason. This had nothing to do with Ben she was sure.

Try as she might, she couldn't distrust this man. He sat across from her smiling comfortingly and she felt a warm glow all over without knowing why. It was time for her to stop jumping from job to job. It was time for Mr Jones to stop grieving for his family. Agatha Higgins recommended him so presumably he had all the right references. And if she went to work for him she just might pick up some pointers on portrait painting . . .

'Very well, Mr Jones,' she all but grinned, 'I'd like very much to come and work for you.'

It was settled then and even Renee, who was full of misgivings when she first heard about it, gave her wholehearted approval once she met Mr Jones. He came for dinner one evening and charmed them all. Renee's boys climbed all over his lap and shared their secrets with him and Jack plied him with fine brandy and good cigars while listening to his entertaining stories about his art classes at the University of Western Australia.

His house in Nedlands, one of Perth's many suburbs, was big and old and comfortable and Danielle had no trouble settling in a week later. He showed her through it with a mixture of pride and embarrassment. The rooms were large and airy, but they lacked something.

'It's missing a woman's touch.' he said softly. 'I remember my wife used to love wild flowers. In bowls, in vases, in jars. They were everywhere.'

Now there was only emptiness, she saw.

Nothing softened the austerity of the bare, colour washed walls. The furniture was sparse and functional. The tables bare. A fine layer of dust lay over everything. Somewhere far back in her mind she remembered Ben's house. She heard herself telling him it was very beautiful. *It's very empty*, he had answered her. She hadn't realised he was a widower at the time. She wondered if this was a quality peculiar to all men who had lost their wives.

Dragging her eyes back to Mr Jones, she shook herself and smiled at him. 'You must miss your wife very much.'

'I do,' he said quietly. 'She was like sunshine.' His face changed slightly. 'My daughter was like moonlight.' Smiling at the analogy, he held out his hand to her. 'Come with me. I'll show you.'

His gallery was at the top of the house. One huge room, it was fitted with a long wide skylight in the sloped ceiling. The floor was bare except for dull splatters of paint here and there. Four big windows had slatted blinds on them, but no curtains. There was an empty fireplace and a sofa and a chair. Strewn across the wide mantel were brushes of every imaginable size and pots and paints. Several easels held half finished paintings and many more canvasses were stacked against the walls. There were tables filled with tubes of colour and more brushes and pens and charcoal, palette knives and pads and drawing tablets.

'It's a bit neglected like the rest of the house,' he said ruefully, glancing around the room and seeing it through Danielle's eyes. 'I don't expect you to clean this room at all.' Picking through several canvasses, he found two small ones and turned them to her. 'This is my wife, Nell.' His voice was quiet, his smile sad.

She had short curly white hair and a gentle lined face. A pretty woman, Danielle thought. Her eyes were as blue as her husband's and they lit up the canvas and her smile was radiant.

'I see what you mean about sunshine,' Danielle said softly.

At once the sadness left his face. Mr Jones beamed and then held out the other painting. 'And this is Elizabeth.'

The portrait of his daughter had a cool arresting quality. Her hair was a shoulder length brunette with rich almost red tones in the soft waves. Her eyes were dark, her bearing regal. She wasn't smiling, but there was devilment lurking in the firm line of her mouth. She wasn't beautiful but there was something in the way she held herself that made Danielle wish she could have known her. Self assurance, she thought. This girl had been loved and she knew it. How sad for her to be dead. She wondered what her husband was like, this son-in-law of Mr Jones' who obviously loved her and had the difficult job of overcoming his own grief and convincing Mr Jones it was time to go on living.

She let out an unsteady breath. 'Moonlight. I can see why you miss them both.'

He smiled and his warm blue eyes studied the unashamed compassion in hers. 'I knew you would understand,' was all he said as he placed the paintings back against the wall.

Danielle found it easy to keep house for this gentle undemanding man. He lived simply, as he said, but she saw that he had a tremendous appreciation for the finer things in life. This appreciation found its expression in his paintings, all intricate perfection and lovely colours and forms and outlines and dainty subtlety.

When he wasn't teaching, he spent long hours reading or walking through the neighbourhood or meeting with his students who knew they were welcome to drop in at any time.

Danielle loved to listen to their conversations. Being college students, they argued not only art, but also a variety of other subjects as well, often becoming deeply philosophical as they sat drinking tea until nearly midnight. She never took part, content just to listen and observe, filling their cups and refilling the plates of scones that always emptied at an astonishing rate. What she didn't understand, Mr Jones patiently explained in simpler terms after the others had gone home. These talks were gentle and informative and Danielle absorbed so much without being aware of it.

As the days passed, Mr Jones' explanations became fewer and she began to offer her own point of view and take part in the discussions. Metaphysics intrigued her, but she found aesthetics more to her taste since it dealt with the study of the nature of beauty in the fine arts. She tried to apply some of the things she learned to her painting, thinking they could only make it better, and without realising it her portraits began to take on a new dimension.

But still something was missing. Portraits were supposed to live, she told herself day after day, standing at her easel after the housework was done. Hers were wooden.

'Don't worry, my dear,' Mr Jones gently encouraged her. 'It will come. The anatomical form and geometrical construction are perfect. I like your contrast of light and shadow. What you need to concentrate on is the movement and direction, the expression and skin tones. Try to capture the character.'

The changing seasons brought changes to Danielle's way of thinking as well. Winter no longer plagued her with the memory of lazy days spent at the beach with Ben. Nor was summer merely the dreaded Christmas holiday season with all Ben's bittersweet connotations. Mr Jones kept her busy and introduced her to new things: music, ballet, the theatre. She even accompanied him on several field trips to art galleries and exhibitions with his students and she was allowed to sit in on some of his classes at the University. With growing poise and sureness, she was able to put Ben out of her mind for longer stretches of time. Only at night when she was alone and everything was silent and still, would his memories come back. She used to torture herself with the futile longing for more than memories, but eventually she learned to accept that this was all she could have and be grateful for it. Ben's memory was part of her. Loving him and losing him the way she did, had made her the person she was. She could never stop loving him, but she did stop longing for him.

If Mr Jones wondered why she was kind

and outgoing to his students and friends, but never would consider dating any of them, he never asked. He respected her privacy and she respected his. Many times she waited for him outside the cemetery gate when he visited his wife's and daughter's graves. He never said anything, but he accepted her silent consolation. She never went with him to visit his son-in-law. He would come home after these visits very quiet and withdrawn, but not melancholy and she wondered if there was some kind of anger or hurt feelings there, but she never asked. It was odd that his son-in-law never visited him, since Mr Jones always seemed to have somebody here. She began to wonder about him. What kind of man could make his wife feel so well loved? She thought again of that cool assured girl in the portrait and wished she could have known her.

Several times she and Mr Jones went north to visit her mother and father and at least once a month they had dinner with Renee and Jack and Tom and Josie. For the first time in her life everything was peaceful and calm and ordered.

One evening, early in December, a year after she had come to work for him, Mr Jones came in and found Danielle hard at work at an easel in his gallery.

'Finished yet?' he grinned, dropping his briefcase on a table and coming around the easel to look. He had become more jaunty lately and his eyes held an irrepressible twinkle. 'I told the school custodian you'd have it finished by tomorrow and he could set it up for me then.'

Danielle dabbed a streak of black on the canvas then stood back, her brow furrowed, looking at her work. Mr Jones wanted her to be included in his student's exhibition for the University's Art Festival and she wanted this to be perfect. There were two landscapes she had already finished and given him for display, but this portrait was to be her *pièce de résistance*. 'What do you think?' she asked in a very small voice.

Mr Jones studied the portrait with intense concentration, barely keeping his excitement contained. In the past year he had nurtured her talent, knowing from the first time he saw her work, that she had tremendous potential. 'I wasn't wrong,' he said almost reverently, his eyes glued to the canvas. 'It has magic.'

She bit her lip and rubbed her forehead with the back of her arm, the brush still clenched in her hand. She was pleased with the compliment, but disappointed that he couldn't see that it still wasn't quite right. 'I don't know,' she said huskily, 'I keep thinking there's something wrong. But I don't know what.' She tilted her head to the side and kept looking at it.

It was Ben, of course. She knew she'd never be able to paint anybody else until she had painted him. Her whole soul was on that canvas. It was in the midnight black of his hair and in the golden glow of his eyes, in the arrogant tilt of his head against a bright and lucid sky. Light was all around him but it seemed to come from him as well. His skin was remote and cool and living and so many times in the dead of night she would creep up here to put her hand to his lips expecting to feel their soft pulsing warmth only to be jolted by the rough texture of cold dried paint. She hadn't forgotten that tiny mole above his right eyebrow. It seemed to mock her now, as did the thin lines of anger bracketing his mouth. His eyes were desolate yet everything else about him was condemning. He lived and breathed a silent bitter disdain.

It was a strange portrait. It told so much yet it told nothing at all.

'Maybe it's the eyes,' Mr Jones said after a moment. 'They're not quite that gold. Add a touch of grey to the outside edge.'

She started to do as he said then stopped dead, her lips opening on an indrawn breath.

She stood stock still, a dark coldness seeping through her before she swung about, confronting him. For an instant there was a look of incredulity on her face then it rapidly lost all colour. 'You know him!'

Mr Jones was utterly still then he smiled with difficulty, clearing his throat and colouring with sudden guilt. 'Danielle,' he said deliberately, 'I can explain——'

Danielle, more and more astonished, kept her eyes fixed on him, her body rigid. Her heart began to pound and her stomach clenched with a curious sinking feeling.

For weeks now he'd watched this portrait take shape. He knew Ben, but he never let on. He never said anything.

The hair at the back of her neck stood on end. Her pulse roared and goosebumps broke out on her skin. 'How do you know Ben?' she said almost savagely.

Tearing his eyes away from her, Mr Jones rubbed his forehead and approached the portrait. He looked at it with deep sadness. A look of lostness was about his mouth and eyes. A long slow breath escaped him. 'He's my son-in-law,' he said quietly.

CHAPTER EIGHT

Stunned, Danielle could only look at him. It was not possible. This had to be some hideous figment of her imagination. Ben couldn't be his son-in-law. Mr Jones' daughter was Elizabeth. And then it hit her. . . . Libby.

As if involuntarily pulled, her eyes went to the portrait sitting on the floor propped up against the wall, to the girl with the cool self assurance, to the girl who knew she had been loved. Something twisted inside her. All this time she had been looking at Ben's wife. Ben's! This was the girl he had loved, had married, had known intimately. It was one thing to picture him with some nebulous woman, but quite another to actually see her. She heard her heart pounding in her ears. Her hands made a futile repudiating gesture as she shivered and flung her brush away, her eyes staring stonily ahead, blind to everything but Ben.

Ben with this girl, holding her, caressing her, loving her. Tears rose in her throat and she swallowed them back savagely. A wild devastating pain swept through her. Mingled with this pain was an overwhelming humiliation. Mr Jones knew, had known all along, that Ben was the man she loved. His son-in-law!

She saw herself talking to him all this past year, discussing her private thoughts and fears, always in the abstract, yet all the while unknowingly telling him all about herself and Ben.

'How could you?' she said through stiff lips, turning her head and dragging her eyes back to his. 'Oh, Mr Jones, how could you?'

He looked at her without speaking. Green fire blazed from her eyes. Her disordered hair escaped from its knot to fall in long brown wisps about her ears and neck. Her pink blouse was rolled up to the elbows and her jeans were paint spattered. She was so different from the first time he had seen her. Then she had been tired, beaten, full of hopelessness. Now she was angry and humiliated, but he knew she would be able to cope with it. Before, she had lived a private solitary existence within her sister's family. Now she was more outgoing. She had more assurance, more self-confidence. This past year with him had opened up a whole new world for her and she knew her place in it. He had helped her to achieve that much.

A slow heavy flush rose in his face and he said softly; 'Ben thought I could help you.'

Hands seemed to be gripping her throat. She shook her head numbly. Angry words rushed to her lips, but looking at him, she could say nothing at all. Ben thought, her heart drummed, Ben thought. Then all at once grief and despair fell on her like a crushing wall. She felt naked, stripped. Ben had known everything all this time. Each time Mr Jones had visited him, he must have been reporting on her. He must have told him all the things she said and thought ... the way she felt.

'I thought you were my friend!' she flung at him.

'I am, Dani.'

She flushed deeply and her eyes flashed with angry humiliation. 'What kind of friend is it who isn't truthful?'

'I never lied to you.'

'You lied by omission!'

'It wasn't intentional.'

She turned to him fully with quiet bitterness. Her mouth thinned. 'I don't believe you.'

He lifted his shoulders in apology. 'I know I should have told you who I was at first, but I didn't think you would come with me if you knew Ben was behind it. So I waited.' He shifted uncomfortably, knowing she was resisting everything he said. 'Ben asked me to take you in and teach you everything I could. As time passed, the opportunity to tell you about him simply never presented itself again. And then it didn't seem important any more. All I could see was your talent. That's all that mattered.' He looked again at Ben's portrait, at all the brooding condemnation and silent disdain in the set of his shoulders, the coldly contemptuous smile, the quiet desolate eyes. 'I wasn't wrong about you,' he said almost reverently, turning back to her. 'You've captured him perfectly. I've seen him like this a hundred times: contemptuous of everything, yet there's always that desolation in him that overrides it. None of my other students have ever caught such emotion on canvas. You have genius.'

Danielle should have been flattered, but all she could feel was a wounded betrayal. She shivered, clenching and unclenching her jaw. 'You never really needed me to keep house for you at all, did you? It was just a ploy to get me to come here.'

A long silence stood between them. He saw her features frozen in despair, but her green eyes were blazing. She was unbendingly still and fierce and rigid. 'Try to understand,' he said gently. 'I was doing this for Ben. He asked me to give you your chance to become a great artist.'

'He was manipulating me.'

'Not manipulating, Dani. He was trying to help you.'

'I don't need any help!'

'Not any more, perhaps, but you did when I first met you.'

'You felt sorry for me, that's all.'

'I did not. I wanted to help you.' He shook his head. 'I needed to help you. I needed you as much as you needed me. Not as a housekeeper but to give my life purpose again.'

'You were wrong not to tell me.'

'I know. And I apologise if I've hurt you.'

'You haven't hurt me,' she said fiercely. 'But you let me hurt you! All this time . . .' her hand flung out wildly, '. . . I was telling you about Ben and you knew it! He's your daughter's husband! Do you have any idea how that makes me feel?'

'Guilty,' he said flatly. 'But there's no reason for it. Nor was there ever any reason for Ben to feel that way. It took me a long time to make him see that. For a year now, I've been talking to him, trying to make him see that he wasn't wrong to love you.'

Something flashed in Danielle's eyes and she half turned away. How could he be saying this? It was so unfair to his daughter. She was dead and couldn't have her say.

'Let me explain,' he said softly.

Her expression didn't change. She clasped her hands in front of her and looked at them as if she wasn't listening, but he knew she was listening intently.

His face softened. 'I worried about Ben when my daughter died. Everything seemed to stop for him. He lost interest in his work. He wouldn't see his son. He shut himself up in his study and refused to talk to anybody for weeks on end. It seemed to me that there was something more than my daughter's death bothering him, but he wouldn't tell me. You know how close he is to his mother. Even she couldn't reach him.'

Danielle unknowingly held her breath and became even more rigid. Of course something more was bothering him. Her! She had made him feel he betrayed Libby by sitting with him in the hospital. Guilt ran through her. She had been the unwitting cause of his problems.

'Then little by little he began to come out of it,' he went on carefully. 'It was Christmastime. He knew his mother loved the season as well as he did. Perhaps more. He told her there was no reason not to celebrate it the way she always had. His sorrow was his alone and shouldn't affect the rest of the family. So she threw her party, thinking somehow it might help him come all the way back to us. I was there,' he said softly. 'And so were you.'

A faint blush began creeping up her neck, but her expression remained stony.

'I saw what happened to you in the hall when that idiot caterer embarrassed you. And I saw how Ben handled it. That was the first inkling I had that you were the missing link. There was something between the two of you. The pieces of the puzzle began falling into place.

Danielle wanted to die.

'I wondered about it for a long time,' he said gently, 'but I never said anything to Ben. I waited. Finally he came to me and told me about you.'

Her heart sank. 'He never was unfaithful to Libby,' she whispered.

'You don't have to tell me that. I know Ben. But there was all that guilt and I couldn't see any reason for it. That's when I agreed to have you come here to me.'

She stiffened. Her whole expression altered and her voice quivered with icy passion. 'To find out what was between Ben and me? Why didn't you just come right out and ask? Why did you have to pretend to be my friend?'

'I didn't pretend, Dani. If I had come to you and told you who I was and asked you about Ben, what would you have told me?'

She clamped her lips together in a thin hard line.

'That's right,' he said softly. 'You would have said nothing. I'm Libby's father, after all. So I went about finding out what I needed to know in a different way.' He looked slightly ashamed, but he managed to shrug it off. 'I'm not saying it was the right way, but between the two of you, I've found out what was troubling Ben.'

She looked desolate. 'Ben despises me. He blames me for him not being with Libby when she died.'

'I know,' he said gently. 'But he's wrong. He was as close to her as they allowed him to be. You had nothing to do with that. You sat with him as any friend would do.'

'I didn't know she was dying.'

'Would it have made a difference?' he asked. 'If you had known, would you have let him wait alone?'

'No,' she said raggedly, looking everywhere but at him. 'I wanted to be with him. I wanted to help him in some way. He looked so . . . unhappy, so . . . helpless.'

'He was. And if his thoughts strayed from my daughter to you at that time, it was no sin. He didn't know she was dying either.'

'But she did die. And it was wrong.'

'No it wasn't. Ben couldn't help feeling the way he did. He loved you. He told me he loved you from the first moment he ever saw you. I don't know why the two of you never married. All I know is when my daughter met him, she was content to pick up the pieces you had left behind. She was there and he was grateful for it.'

A whimper of pain sounded deep in her throat and she turned her face away. Ben, Ben, her heart cried, but all she could see was him wrapped in Libby's arms. All her worst imaginings when she first heard about his marriage paraded again before her eyes: Ben loving this beautiful girl, lying with her, his hands on her body, his lips on her mouth.

Intense pity rose in Mr Jones and profound understanding. He took her ice cold hands in his and led her, stiffly resisting, to the sofa and made her sit beside him. 'Elizabeth knew about you,' he said quietly, chafing her hands. At her stiffening jerk, he went on hurriedly, 'Oh, not in any personal way, mind you. She just knew your name was Danielle and Ben had loved you. Someone in his family mentioned it, I think. She was too much a pragmatist to let it bother her, though. She knew there would be a tiny little corner of his heart reserved for you and she never trespassed on it. She simply accepted it and went on with the business of loving him.'

Danielle hung her head in shame. If their situations were reversed, she knew she wouldn't be that magnanimous. Her eyes strayed to Libby's portrait once more.

'She's never been your rival,' he went on, his eyes softening as he too looked at the portrait. 'She meant a great deal to Ben, but she never took your place in his affections. He loved you. He loved my daughter in a different way and it was enough for her.

'No!' She didn't understand how he could say this so calmly. This was his daughter he was talking about. How could he be so disloyal? Why wasn't he denouncing her for coming between Libby and Ben? How could he take her into his home and be as kind as he was and teach her so many things and help her in so many ways? She had hurt Libby in the worst possible way without meaning to.

'Yes!' He almost crushed her hands in his and compelled her to look at him. 'This is what Ben has been grappling with ever since she died. And you as well, in your own way. He felt he betrayed Elizabeth because he never stopped loving you.'

'Did he tell you that?' she said, aghast.

'He didn't have to. I know Ben. He's an unusually sensitive man and sophistication is still new to him. From the things he said, I heard a lot more than he was telling me.'

'Oh, why did it have to be Libby who died?' she groaned in despair. 'Why not me?'

'Stop that right now,' he gently rebuked her. 'That's not something that can be questioned. Everything happens for a reason and all we can do is try to make the best of it.'

'But Libby died! How can anything good be made of that?'

'By looking at it from a different perspective,' he said softly. 'Dying isn't always bad. Sometimes living can be worse. The doctors told me she never would have been able to raise her son if she had lived. Her heart was too frail . . . she would have been an invalid . . . bedridden . . .' his voice faded away to almost nothing. 'Ben already regretted marrying her. He didn't need that added burden.'

'Regretted?' Her eyes widened and she caught her breath and held it.

'It wasn't long after he married that I noticed that look about him.'

The dull red blood of shame began to creep into her face. She was appalled by the thoughts trying to crowd in on her. The inference of what he was saying shouldn't make her feel good. She shifted uncomfortably, ill at ease and troubled. Confusion shimmered in her eyes.

'It's all right,' Mr Jones smiled gently, looking steadily at her. 'Don't be ashamed of what you're feeling. Loving Ben as you do, it's only natural for you to feel almost glad that he couldn't love his wife the way he loved you.'

His understanding and acceptance only made her feel worse. This was his daughter he was talking about. 'How can you be so disloyal to Libby?' she choked.

He leaned forward a little closer to his daughter's portrait as if trying to find the right words to say, gentle words, reasonable words. 'I'm not being disloyal really. I knew my daughter. You didn't. She got her pragmatism from me. What is, is. So we accept it. If Ben regretted marrying her, Elizabeth was never aware of it,' he said quietly. 'He was always gentle and attentive to her. He became very adept at hiding his feelings. But I'm a portrait painter. I'm used to reading expressions. I knew something was wrong at once. I just didn't know what. I waited for years to hear what I suspected— that there was another woman somewhere in the background. Instead, there was never a hint of it. Ben simply threw himself into his work.'

Tears began to roll soundlessly down Danielle's cheeks.

'The story's not all that unique when you think about it.' His smile twisted. 'And it isn't all that unhappy either. His hard work paid off. Ben made a fortune and Elizabeth enjoyed it. She never knew what drove him. She simply accepted it. She never had to put on a false front and act the part of the happy housewife. She was happy and Ben was kind to her.'

Danielle moved slightly and spoke in a dry spent tone. 'It could have been better for her, but I came between them. I was wrong. Oh, how I wish I hadn't done that.'

He released her hands and regarded her with quiet but passionate earnestness. 'You did nothing, Danielle. And neither did Ben. The two of you couldn't help loving each other. It's taken me all this time to make Ben see that. He finally has. Now I have to convince you.'

'You don't understand.' She stood up and faced him with trembling calm. 'The problem isn't admitting I love Ben. That's never been a secret to anyone. The problem is accepting the way I hurt him and Libby.'

'But I just told you, she never was hurt.'

'She was, don't you see? The reason I never married Ben was because he wasn't good enough for me!' Angry red colour filled her face.

Mr Jones' eyes widened as he tried to understand her reasoning. 'I find it hard to believe you could ever think that way. That doesn't sound like you at all. I've met your mother several times. That sounds more like something she would say.'

'My mother pointed out his unsuitability,' she said raggedly, 'but in the end I chose to believe it.' She hung her head in shame. 'But I didn't tell Ben that at the time. I simply left him without any real explanation. I made him think I lost interest, that I didn't love him any more.' She flung her hands out angrily. 'I didn't have the decency to end it cleanly, to set him free, to allow him to love somebody else.'

His face changed then and his eyes softened with sudden complete understanding. He rested his hands on his knees and watched the frightened pain reflected in her eyes, pain for all the wasted time when she couldn't change anything, no matter how hard she tried. He knew she was suffering the agonies of the reserved, which could be so much more poignant than the loudly emotional.

'You're wrong, you know,' he said gently. 'The only one who was never free to love again was you. Ben might have been exclusively in your thoughts all these years, but once you told him goodbye, he eventually got over the hurt and came to accept it as final. That's the missing link, the piece of the puzzle I've been looking for. Don't you see? Ben loved you, but he accepted the futility of it and got on with his life and made something of it. You didn't. You've been dwelling on the hurt all this time, living with your regrets, probably first blaming your mother, then turning it all in on yourself. But you're wrong. That part of your life is over and done with. You loved Ben and lost him. You just never let him go. Now its all different. Now there's hope. Now is the right time for a new beginning for both of you.'

Her eyes clung to his face in despair. Slow hot tears brimmed and silently spilled over.

With the utmost gentleness and tenderness, he stood and folded her stiff resisting body in his arms, letting her bury her face in his chest while he patted her back comfortingly. 'I know. It isn't going to be easy. There's been a lot of misunderstanding. Ben's one of a kind and you've loved him a long time,' he soothed. 'But try to chalk it up to human frailty. You're older and wiser now. Take a look at what happened and see it for what it was: two people simply too young to understand the kind of love you had. You're both different people now. It's time to put past hurts and regrets behind you. It's only by letting go of the past, that we can take hold of the future.'

Danielle couldn't see any future—with or without Ben. 'It's hopeless!' she cried. 'I've left it too late. Ben's changed. If I went to him now, he would think it was because of his money or his position. He wouldn't think I love him for himself. No, Mr Jones. It would never work. He doesn't want to see me no matter what you say, no matter what he might have told you.'

She clung to him for a long time full of rage and love and hatred, full of longing and loathing and yearning and self-disgust. She sighed so deeply her thin body was wrenched with it and Mr Jones could only stand with her while she worked it out herself.

All through dinner and on into the evening she felt his sympathetic eyes on her. They didn't speak of Ben again, yet he was there between them, uppermost in both their thoughts. Danielle did the dishes and somehow put the finishing touches to Ben's portrait before going to bed.

Sleep was the furthest thought from her

mind as she lay between the sheets, staring at the shadows on the ceiling. She couldn't help but go over everything that had been said in detail. And she relived her mortification all over again. Utterly depressed and miserable, she wanted to believe Mr Jones, but she knew he was wrong. There was no hope for a new beginning. The time would never be right. The only thing left was to change her perspective and put Ben behind her. Up until this time she never thought of him as anything other than the love of her life. Now she had to try to see him as just a man, someone she had loved and lost.

As disconcerting as it was, she forced herself to acknowledge that Ben Harper, as rich and powerful and eminently successful as he was now, most likely was no longer interested in her. After all, she reasoned, he had been a widower for more than a year and that was plenty of time for him to have found someone else, someone suitable to his way of life. Danielle would never fit in. She was ordinary. He was not. He was far beyond her now.

But still, a niggling little thought fluttered in the back of her mind, a loose end that bothered her. She hadn't seen him in all this time, but somehow he had made himself responsible for her welfare. He had arranged for Mr Jones to take her into his home and teach her. Something fiercely independent and proud welled up inside her. She wouldn't tolerate his pity or charity or whatever it was. If she was letting him go, she had to do it completely.

CHAPTER NINE

DANIELLE reluctantly made her way through the long cool halls of the University the next evening. She hadn't wanted to come, but she had promised Mr Jones and she couldn't back out now. Nervously straightening her dress, a knee length dark red jersey with short sleeves and a draping cowl neckline, she patted her hair into place. Several long wisps escaped from her topknot to trail on to her shoulders and try as she might, she couldn't confine them and make them stay where they belonged.

Some of the students and guests were already assembled in the main exhibition room, standing in animated groups, waving and calling out to her when they saw her hovering in the doorway. She smiled back, trying to look more at ease than she felt. She was afraid Ben would be here tonight and she wasn't prepared to face him yet.

Brilliant, glowing canvasses were everywhere. Some were mounted on the wide pale walls and some were on easels angled to catch a certain light. There were portraits and landscapes and one very moving seascape imprisoning forever the passion and power of the artist who painted it.

Mr Jones was talking to a short plump woman and Danielle knew he was proudly describing the hard work the woman's daughter had done all year. The girl stood deferentially behind her mother, but Mr Jones drew her out and praised her so lavishly it brought a blush to her face. There was so much more involved than just putting paint on canvas and he took advantage of every opportunity to acknowledge it.

As more people began to cluster around him, he took them for a closer inspection, enthusiastically pointing out some of the finer nuances of the art. After a while the murmurs of admiration and respect for such a dedicated teacher became outright compliments and Danielle felt a curious sinking feeling in her stomach at the way he nodded, humbly accepting their tribute.

He was an inspiration to everyone who had the good fortune to study under him. Everyone knew that. Yet all year, whenever she had tried to thank him for what he was teaching her, he wouldn't hear of it. She knew she never would have come this far if it hadn't been for him, but he never listened when she tried to tell him so.

Because of Ben. It had to be. Everything always came back to him. She would bet anything that Ben had paid him to teach her. That was why he wouldn't let her thank him.

Ben was responsible for giving her father a new lease on life. By making it possible for him to overcome his drinking problem, he managed to sweep away all her mother's worries at the same time. In this same silent underhanded way he had given Danielle this opportunity to develop her talent while learning from the best, making sure she lived in a good home without having to worry about earning her living.

She should have been grateful. She was, in a way. But that gratitude was mixed up with bitterness, for Ben, for Mr Jones, most of all for her own ignorance and gullibility. Ben had not been honest with her. At the very least Mr Jones should have told her. Why hadn't she realised he never really needed her? It was only a token job with an outrageous salary and she had no doubt where that salary came from. What Ben didn't know yet, was that he was going to get back every penny. Her expenses had been few this past year. Most of the money had been saved and she looked forward to throwing it all back in his face. She had too much stubborn pride to willingly accept

anything from him now. She threw an
accusing look at his portrait mounted on the
wall and turned her back on it, trying not to
despair. She would get over him. She had to.

Two hours dragged by before she told
herself Ben wasn't going to come tonight. It
almost made her sick with anti-climax. Some
urgent business must have prevented him
from leaving his office, she reasoned, not
knowing whether to be relieved or angry. She
had worked herself into a fine state of tension
for nothing. Chiding herself for being so
mixed up in her emotions, she kept her eyes
resolutely away from Ben's portrait. Mr Jones
had to have told him about it and arranged
for him to be here. Why else would he have
been so adamant that she finish it for tonight?

Pinning a smile to her face, she slowly
made her way to a long table containing
refreshments at the far end of the room and
sipped a glass of punch. Some part of her still
half expected to see Ben, yet she knew she
wouldn't. It was too late. Some people were
beginning to leave already.

When a sudden sliver of cold traced its way
down her spine, everything inside her froze.
Even without seeing him she knew only one
person could make her react like that. Ben
had finally come. Turning, she saw him
before he saw her. He was stepping back in

the doorway to let a beautiful dark haired woman precede him into the room. They both were dressed in evening clothes, Ben in a dark trim fitting suit and white shirt and tie and the woman in a midnight blue lace dress with a daring plunging neckline.

Danielle drank in the sight of him. Her eyes fixed on his face as if she couldn't have enough of the seeing. In spite of herself, everything in her strained towards him. For the past year she had been living with his memory and now he was here. Only the width of the room separated them. He was living, breathing, flesh and blood. She thought she had captured him so well on canvas, but she saw at once how pale an imitation it was. He was so much more— bigger, bolder, more handsome. The shape of his face, the grace of his body, the impact of his magnetism held her, and a kind of reluctant and angry awe ran through her.

No man had a right to be that handsome. He was leaner than she remembered, and more tanned. The tiny lines radiating from the corners of his eyes were deeper. Hollows were in his cheeks and bluish shadows beneath his eyes. But he was still Ben. His upper lip was a firm straight line, the lower one fuller, wider. His hair was black and shining and falling rakishly across his brow.

She tore her eyes away and forced herself to look at the woman with him. Crushing back a rush of jealousy that flooded her, she steeled herself to keep from shivering. This was just what she needed: to see Ben with the beautiful woman who must be part of his life now. This alone should give her the perspective she was looking for. Now she would get over him once and for all.

The woman was striking. Tall and slender, she was a perfect complement to him. Together they looked chic and coolly sophisticated, at ease in any situation. While Ben was tanned, she had pearly white, unblemished skin. Her hair was long and loose, falling in shining dark waves far down her back. Her dark eyes held calmness and gentleness and reflected an inner serenity Danielle could never hope to find.

She watched the woman gently smile up at Ben and murmur something before turning and walking towards a group of people clustered around a vibrant pulsing landscape. Seeing Ben's assessing eyes follow her made Danielle physically sick. This woman wasn't possessive, where Danielle would have been. She was leaving Ben to his own devices and Danielle felt a sudden stab of mortification remembering how she had been shy and clinging and probably very boring to a man of his worldly experience.

She felt a prickling behind her eyelids and a sob deep inside her, but somehow she quashed both. What was the matter with her? Had she no pride? No self-respect? No pain at her own humiliation? She realised she was trembling and quickly put down the glass she was holding. She had to get out of here before she made a fool of herself.

As unobtrusively as possible she inched her way along the wall, concealed by the crowd yet able to keep Ben in her line of vision, watching him move away from the door to skim over the paintings with a faintly bored air. She wondered what his reaction would be when he saw her portrait of him, but didn't stay to watch.

Once out in the hallway, she automatically searched for a telephone to call a taxi. She felt sick, physically nauseated, torn to pieces by emotions she didn't want to identify. Oh why, she thought shakily, digging into the bottom of her handbag to find coins for the 'phone, why couldn't she hate him? Why couldn't she despise him? Why did it only take one look at him to make all her resolve fly out the window, all her safe tidy world come crashing down around her ears? She didn't want to love Ben any more. Would she ever get over him?

'What's the matter, Dani?'

She almost dropped her handbag. Stiffening with a jerk, she looked back over her shoulder to the tall young man in blue jeans who stood behind her in the dim hallway. 'Oh! Jim! You startled me,' she said breathlessly relieved this was one of Mr Jones' favourite students and not Ben.

'Mr Jones saw you leave and said you looked a little upset. He sent me after you. Is everything all right?' His bright blue eyes skimmed over her ashen face.

'Oh ... everything's fine,' she hurried to reassure him. 'I just ...' She lifted her shoulders helplessly. 'I was ready to go home and Mr Jones looked like he would be a while yet, so I was just calling a taxi.'

'You don't have to do that.' He gave her a sudden wicked smile. 'I'll take you home if you'll let me. How many times have I asked you out before?'

She bit her lip. 'Jim——'

'Don't refuse me, Dani.' He held up his hands. 'I know you don't want to get involved. You've told me that often enough. Just let me take you home.'

She kept glancing past him, afraid Ben might suddenly appear. 'All right. Thank you. But just a lift home.'

His smile became rueful. 'Let's go tell Mr Jones.'

'You go. I'll meet you outside.'

He took a step towards her. 'If something's wrong——'

'No! No, it isn't,' she rushed. If she went back in there she would run into Ben and she didn't want to risk that. 'I'm just a bit warm, that's all. And besides, Mrs Wright has been dogging my footsteps all evening. You wouldn't want me to get stuck with her, would you?'

He grimaced, thinking of the assistant professor who had a penchant for reminiscing about the good old days more than twenty years before. Her favourite story was about the time hospitable Perthians switched on every light bulb in town to greet America's first orbiting astronaut, John Glenn, as he sped through the night overhead. It was something everyone knew, but she could ramble on for hours about how Perth came to be called the 'City of Lights'.

'All right, Dani. Give me five minutes. I'll meet you outside in the car park.'

She smiled her thanks and hurriedly turned.

As soon as she was outside she began to breathe easier. She wasn't ready to see Ben yet. Her emotions were too much in turmoil.

Maybe she would just mail him a certified cheque or have Mr Jones give him all his money back. She would have to think about the best way to do it. But not now. She might say things she would forever regret. She was too upset to think straight.

The long soft December twilight was folding itself over the city, promising a beautifully peaceful night. The air was warm and richly scented, the breeze wafting through the flower beds on the University grounds, mingling and mixing the tangy scent of grass and vines and wildflowers. Within a few minutes her tension began to leave her and she stood next to Jim's car waiting for him, looking up into the soothing enchantment of the starry sky.

'Waiting for me, Dani?' The familiar voice she least wanted to hear came from behind her as low and as softly velvet as the night.

Her heart lurched and suddenly began to hammer. She clenched her hands at her sides and didn't turn around, more aware of him than ever. Her eyes squeezed tightly shut in despair. 'Ben,' she breathed achingly. 'I . . . no . . .' She shook herself, '. . . that is, I'm waiting for Jim Sinclair. He's going to take me home.'

'Let me take you.'

'No!' she said too quickly, then nervously tried to control her stammer. 'I mean . . .

thank you anyway, but Jim should be back any minute. He went to tell Mr Jones ...' Her voice trailed away.

Ben's hands descended on her shoulders, paralysing her instantly. Slowly turning her to face him, he looked straight into her face before shaking his head. His eyes were darkly gold and full of pain. 'Don't you know your running days are over? You'll never run away from me again.'

She could feel panic rising to her throat, but she gave a ghost of a laugh and looked everywhere but at him. 'I'm not running away from you, Ben. You just startled me, that's all. You're the last person I expected to see here tonight. I didn't know you were interested in art. Are you just now coming? I'm afraid you're a bit late. People are beginning to leave already——'

The tightening of his hands stopped her. 'I'll take you home,' he said softly, his eyes reflecting everything she was feeling but trying so hard to hide. Almost as if he couldn't stop himself, he gently stroked the sides of her neck where her pulse pounded heavily. His fingers rested on her shoulders, his thumbs sliding beneath the draping neckline of her dress to the smooth bones of her throat gently moving up and down the pale flesh. 'It's time we talked.'

A throbbing awareness shuddered through her and she couldn't get her breath. 'No.'

'Dani,' he said thickly, 'don't say no.' His hands curled almost of their own volition and he drew her resistingly against him, moulding her to his finely trembling body. He pressed her face into his wide shoulder where she was tantalised by the elusive scent of him, clean and warm and male. She could feel the harsh unsteady rhythm of his heart beating against her cheek as he just held her there for a long minute. 'Kiss me,' he commanded huskily into her hair. 'Love me. Cleanse me of this devil that's driving me out of my mind.'

And then suddenly he lost his control. He was kissing her over and over again, fierce in his possession, his lips against her throat and her neck and her mouth, his hands dislodging the pins in her hair, tangling in its flowing thickness then moving restlessly up and down the long pliant length of her spine. He held her and caressed her and loved her, his touch moving on her like the hot lick of flames.

She couldn't resist him. She didn't even think of it. At the first touch of his lips she was lost in a blaze of longing that couldn't be denied. Her hands were feverish on his warm and willing body. Somehow several of his shirt buttons were undone and she slipped her fingers inside, curling them into his skin, feeling the bunching muscles of his chest. Everything around her receded. There was only Ben in this starry night, only the feel of him, the sound of his urgent murmurs deep in his throat, the tough of his hard body pressing against every inch of her yielding softness. There was only this sweet weakening throb of urgency and submission and possession.

His hands were at her waist, warm and exquisitely heavy. They moved to her ribs fiercely at first then gentling, slowly inching upward as if he was afraid he would hurt her. They closed over her breasts, cupping, stroking through the thin slippery material of her dress until he felt them harden, filling his hands, swelling with need. His mouth plundered hers, tasting, touching, probing until she was whimpering deep in her throat.

Breathing hard, Ben slowly raised his head, his leaping gold eyes locked on hers for long pulsing seconds. She was lost in them. 'Dani——'

Two teenagers passed by on bicycles and gave an ear splitting wolf whistle and someone close behind them cleared his throat. Danielle blinked dazedly, suddenly becoming aware of where she was. Dragging herself out of his arms, she smoothed her dress with jerky hands and self-consciously tried to restore some kind of order to her hair. She was glad of the darkness hiding her deep red blush.

'Sorry to interrupt,' Jim said coolly.

She murmured something inaudible.

'I'm taking her home, Jim,' Ben said with a decidedly ragged edge to his voice, his eyes still fastened on hers.

'But——'

'No!' she broke in. Oh, how had she let this happen? she berated herself. She had to end this before it started again. She must. She had no defence against him. Using Jim wasn't what she intended to do, but as long as he was here . . . 'I'm going with you, Jim.'

Ben's fists clenched. 'Please, Dani!'

She could only look at him, her soul in her eyes. She wanted to stay, to love him, to never let him go. 'No,' she forced herself to whisper.

Jim opened his car door and somehow she settled herself in the front seat, never taking her eyes off Ben. Her heart twisted at his look of anguish. Everything in her strained to stay, rebelled at leaving, but she had to clamp down on her emotions. She had to leave him now. It was the only way to save herself from more heartache later on. If she was ever going to get over him, distance was her only weapon. Their love never would work. It wasn't the right time for them. It would never be the right time. That was in the past. They were two very different people now and they couldn't go back. He belonged with that beautiful woman in the blue lace dress she had seen earlier.

Jim put his car in gear and drove away and she forced herself to wipe out this last picture of Ben forever from her memory. She didn't want to think of him as being vulnerable, of him standing there without moving, looking utterly defeated and wretched and worn. She had to leave him. There really was no other choice. Silent tears stood in her eyes before rolling down her face when Ben finally dissolved into an indistinct blur in the distance.

Jim drove on in silence. For a good ten minutes he said nothing. Then he turned down a quiet street and parked under a rustling eucalyptus tree, staring straight ahead into the darkness. 'Want to tell big brother Jim all about it?' he said quietly.

Danielle couldn't say anything. Her throat suddenly felt full of hot wax.

After a minute he reached out and pulled her into his arms, letting her bury her face in his shirt front. 'There, there,' he soothed awkwardly. 'I always wondered who my competition was. There had to be somebody, you were always so distant. I should have known it was Ben Harper.'

She wanted to ask how he knew but couldn't get the words out.

'I saw the portrait you painted ...' He patted her back. 'Is that why Ben never came to Mr Jones' house any more? Did you two have a lover's quarrel?'

She sobbed into his shirt but couldn't answer.

'Ben was always there before,' he went on after a long pause. 'Ben and Libby. Funny, Mr Jones never called her that although all the rest of us did. It was always Elizabeth with him. As if she were a queen. Ben treated her like one, that's for sure. And Mr Jones was grateful for it. But I never could understand how the two of them ever got together in the first place. She was a big girl, tall, you know? And on the heavy side. They just never looked right together.'

'Please ... I don't want to hear.'

'I'm not being unkind. And I'm not saying anything a lot of us haven't said before. It's just that when I saw you with Ben tonight, I suddenly realised how right you looked in his arms. Libby never looked that way.' He grinned crookedly. 'I must be out of my mind. I should be pleading my own case, not Ben's. How many times have I asked you to marry me? I knew there was some man in your past. I just didn't know it was Ben. I haven't got a prayer, have I?'

She clung to him helplessly, knowing she was wrong to use his friendship like this, but she was unable to stop herself. At least once a month Jim had asked her to marry him. Usually it was in front of Mr Jones and she thought he was joking but gradually she realised he was serious. She liked him well enough in a brotherly sort of way, but she could never consider marriage. He was a steady person, charming and open and warm. She knew with him she would have peace and harmony and a different kind of happiness. But she couldn't do it. It would be unfair to him. Every time she closed her eyes, it would be Ben's arms around her, Ben's lips on hers, Ben's passion lifting her to heights she never knew existed.

'You love him very much, don't you?' Jim said quietly.

'No,' she choked, shuddering. Maybe if she said it often enough she would convince herself.

His mouth quirked and he gave an exaggerated sigh, accepting defeat with good grace. 'Ah well, the path to true love is never smooth.' With a tact that was so much a part of him, he gave her a cheerful smile. 'How about slipping off somewhere with me and having a drink or two? Soothe your nerves and all that.'

'Oh Jim,' she said wretchedly, 'I know I'm being ungrateful, but would you please just take me home? I wouldn't be very good company right now.'

He sighed again, a real one this time, and smiled sadly. 'All right. Home it is.' He gave her a big brotherly hug and set her away from him. 'If there's something, anything, I can do for you, Dani, all you have to do is say the word.'

She gave him a watery smile. 'Thank you, Jim. I don't deserve to have a friend like you.'

'Sure you do. We're mates, right?'

'Mates,' she said softly, thinking only of Ben.

CHAPTER TEN

THE moonlight dappled the front lawn as Danielle stood on the walk watching Jim drive away. She refused to let him see her to the door and stood for a long time just soaking up the warm Australian night. Her eyes turned to the golden blossoms of the wattle blooming wildly at the side of the house and she had to smile at the flannel flower and fringed lily she had finally coaxed to grow. Mr Jones' garden was sadly neglected before she came. Now there were flowers everywhere, even the red and green Kangaroo paw, Western Australia's floral emblem, and her favourite, the dainty and delicate rock lily.

The breeze hummed in her ears, the soothing scent of wild flowers filled her senses and gradually a kind of peace began to steal over her. She turned and let herself into the house. A lamp was softly lit on a small table to welcome her. She couldn't help but look around the silent empty rooms and remember how they were before she came. Unconsciously her backbone straightened and her chin came up determinedly high. This was a home now because of her. She had made it that way and she was proud of it. There were bowls of flowers on the shining tables and books on the shelves and delicate woodcarvings she had unearthed from a box in the back of a cupboard.

It was a contented atmosphere she had managed to produce and she pictured Mr Jones as she had seen him so many times during the year: seated on the sofa, smiling and relaxed, smoking his pipe, a book open on his knee, students grouped around him on the floor and sprawled on every available chair.

She wouldn't regret coming here to help him, even if he hadn't really needed her. She had set out to do something and she had done it to the best of her ability. But now it was time to leave, to go on to something else. She had outlived her usefulness, overstayed her welcome. The pain of loss and regret began to splinter through her and she took a deep breath, fighting it back, hating the feeling of being so very much alone and vulnerable and forever on the outside looking in.

Ben kept trying to crowd into her mind, but she fought him off too. The way she had left him tonight shattered her, but she wouldn't let herself think about it. Somehow

she would get over the bittersweet re-
membrance of his passion, the exquisite feel
of his body against hers, the heady taste of
his soul stirring kisses. Oh, who was she
kidding? She was made for him. He was the
other half of her soul. How could she keep on
denying it?

Too late, she told herself over and over.
She had had her chance and lost it. It hadn't
been the right time then and it wasn't now
and no amount of dwelling on it would
change it. She had to get over him. He
belonged to Libby once and now he belonged
to some woman in a blue lace dress. There
was no sense trying to hang on to someone
who was never hers in the first place.

Blinking back the dry sting of tears, she
restlessly paced the floor as if to outrun her
thoughts. She picked up a book and put it
down again, turned on the television and
then turned it off and finally with a sound of
disgust, decided not to wait up for Mr Jones
after all. She couldn't talk to him tonight. He
would be exhilarated from the success of his
festival and she would only drag him down
and that wouldn't be fair.

Going to her room, she tried to empty her
mind so she could fall asleep, but it was
impossible. If only she had something to
keep herself occupied. She didn't want to

think of Ben. A long hot soak in the tub should have helped, but after an hour all she had to show for it was shrivelled skin and lips that were turning blue from the rapidly cooling water and eyes that were red from the tears finding their way out of her.

She pulled on a long cotton nightgown and paced the floor of her room. Where would she go? What would she do? Would there every be a place for her? Ben. Ben. Ben. His handsome face kept insinuating itself into her memory, his smile, his gentleness, his inaccessibility. Her place was nowhere near him. He was beyond her, lost to her.

Sleep was impossible so she didn't even try. Barefoot, she threw a thin bathrobe across her shoulders and started to the gallery. Maybe painting would absorb her and help her pull herself together. She had no idea what her subject would be. She only knew she had to do something to keep busy.

Everything was silent and still at the top of the stairs. Her steps started to slow and became almost faltering when she came closer to the great echoing gallery with its dim furniture and piled canvasses and dusky laden shadows. Her breath seemed to stop in her throat and her heart began to beat faster. She reached the doorway and saw the soft glow of a lamp as if someone was waiting here for her. Ice prickled along her spine, tingling all through her. For a moment she couldn't go on. Her legs began to tremble. There was no sound, only a waiting hush and the distant booming echo of her heartbeat thick in her ears. Then she knew she was not alone.

Libby's portrait had been moved from against the wall. It sat on an easel in the centre of the room. The cool painted eyes beckoned and drew her closer and then she saw Ben.

Seated in a chair facing the portrait, he slowly turned and looked at her.

She couldn't read the look on his face. She could only see his rigid handsome features, his lips with their inflexible bluish line, his unreadable gold eyes, so brilliant, yet so guarded.

'Go away, Ben,' she pleaded, her desire to cry nearly choking her. She swallowed convulsively. Let me start getting over you again.

'I'm not going anywhere until we talk,' he said softly, slowly, getting to his feet. 'I told you, your running days are over.' His jacket and tie had been discarded and the buttons of his snowy white shirt were open halfway down his chest.

'We have nothing to talk about.'

'I think we have.' He looked at her face so strangely white and fixed except for a quivering at the corners of her lips. Her eyes, swollen from crying, were deeply burning emeralds, starved and passionate and full of grief and love.

She shook her head from side to side, her eyes never moving from his.

He extended a hand but she took a step backward without a sound. If he touched her, she knew she would be lost.

'I love you, Dani. I've always loved you.'

Her eyes widened and involuntarily flew to Libby's portrait.

He followed her look and lifted his shoulders helplessly. 'I loved Libby, too, but in a different way. Can you understand that?'

After a minute she shook her head again and her mouth trembled. Mr Jones tried to explain it, but she hadn't understood him either. 'No,' she said raggedly.

Pain twisted his mouth and he took a deep breath. 'When you left me seven years ago, I thought you didn't love me any more. I thought you stopped caring. I couldn't stand it. You left and took everything beautiful with you. The world became a dark, cold place for me.' His voice, so low and carefully controlled, suddenly wobbled and she felt a sickening lurch inside her. 'I was lonely and afraid and abandoned. I hated myself then, Dani, for becoming a nuisance to you——'

She turned away uttering an agonised cry and burying her face in her hands.

'Don't,' he said unevenly, coming behind her and putting his arms around her, his eyes darkening with emotion.

She was unaware of him. She was so swallowed up with remorse. How could she have done that to him, made him feel that way? How?

'Dani,' he said when her sobs were quieter. He turned her to face him, keeping her in the warm, secure circle of his arms, resting his cheek against the top of her head. 'I'm not telling you this to make you feel bad, but to explain what I was like when I met Libby.'

His body quivered against the entire length of hers and when she lifted her face from her hands, it was wet and pinched and flaming. She could only look at him in wordless anguish.

'She was good to me,' he said. 'She made me feel worth something again.'

Her mouth trembled more and more. Then all the anguish she had been trying to control suddenly fell in on her with unendurable torture. 'Oh, Ben!'

'She never asked anything of me,' he went on. 'She was content just to be near me. We worked together in the same company and I saw her every day. You might say we simply drifted together. I asked her out to dinner and got to know her mother and father. After a while I began to think of her as the calm after the storm.'

She shuddered. Yes, Danielle had been the storm in his life, the cyclone who disrupted everything. She blew in, then left him tossed and blown and reeling in her wake. He needed Libby and she was there for him in a way Danielle never was.

Ben couldn't help himself. He reached out and tentatively traced the strained lines of her face, feeling her skin tighten under his exploring fingers. He bent and his lips brushed her forehead in a passionless kiss, cautiously, as if she might suddenly shatter in his hands.

Her eyes were huge and stricken and her hands fluttered whitely at her sides before settling at his waist then clinging tightly to the strength of him, afraid she might fall if she didn't hold on. 'Oh, Ben. Ben!' she cried into his chest.

He held her for long minutes, savouring the feel of her against the hard power of his body.

'I'm so sorry,' she choked.

'You have nothing to be sorry for.'

'Yes I do. I hated Libby all these years.

She was good to you and I hated her.'

He sighed softly. 'I understand. But I think if you could have known her, you would have liked her.'

'You don't understand,' she said raggedly. 'I didn't want to like her. I couldn't bear the thought of her having you. You were mine. I always thought of you that way. You belonged to me. You were the other half of my soul. I used to imagine how it would be, calling myself your wife, living with you, loving you. With our children. We would have a lot of them. And they'd all look like you. Can you imagine what it did to me when I heard you were married? I couldn't stand the thought of you with someone else.' Her lips shook and huge tears flooded her eyes. 'Someone else who had the right to love you, to share everything with you, to know everything about you, every facet of your personality, your gentleness, your sensitivity, your very goodness. I hated her for it. And then I hated you.'

She wasn't prepared for his smile, tremulous and tender.

'Dani,' he said softly, almost pleadingly, 'I do understand. Don't you think I felt the same way about you? I loved you in the same way. But don't you remember? When you left me, I never tried to stop you.'

A quiver ran through her before she stiffened and blinked unsteadily. Her lashes were spiky and wet with tears. That was true. In all this time she had forgotten that. When she thought back, she remembered his lack of surprise when she told him it was over. She suddenly realised he had been expecting it. He accepted it calmly, resignedly, almost— relieved.

'No,' he said softly, reading everything in her face. 'I loved you and wanted you then. I love you and want you now.'

She tried to pull away from him but he firmly tightened his arms, moving his lips on her hair, rubbing his cheek against it, keeping her close against his body. 'It was a mistake we both made,' he said quietly. 'We were too young. There was your mother . . .'

'She thought she knew what was best for me.'

'I know. And that's where my pride came in. You chose her over me. If you didn't think I was good enough, I wasn't going to try to convince you. I simply let you go.'

'You knew?' Her face burned.

'I had a pretty fair idea that's what it was. I knew your mother never cared for me or my family. For a long time I hated her for it and then I hated you for listening to her. I told myself I would show up the people who didn't want me. I plotted for years. That's the thing that kept me going. It drove me. And then it finally happened. Your father came to me on his knees needing my help. I had it all. Revenge was mine!'

His mouth twisted. 'Then it was Christmas-time and there you were, a servant kneeling at my feet and everything changed. That wasn't what I wanted at all. I couldn't go through with what I had planned. I had to help your mother and father, not hurt them. I was going to get rid of all of you once and for all, but instead, I arranged for your father to be rehabilitated. You can't imagine what I felt when I saw you like that. You were so abject, yet so proud. Oh, Dani!' His mouth helplessly sought hers and he groaned deep in his throat. 'How could I even contemplate hurting you? I must have been out of my mind!'

His body surged into hers. All his anguish spilled over as he clung to her with the desperation of a drowning man. His powerful arms crushed her and she could feel his raw hunger and aching need and flaring passion.

Her head whirled and her whole body sprang to life. He was so beautiful, so vulnerable, and he loved her. He was shaking, his powerful body racked by con-vulsive shudders making her shatteringly aware of the way his body fit so perfectly to hers, the way his heart was hammering, the way his breath tortured his throat. And all the while he was raining kisses on her forehead and cheeks and hair, anywhere his lips could reach.

Excruciating desire stabbed at her. She wanted to touch him as freely as he was touching her, lovingly, fiercely, desperately. Somehow she loosened his shirt, then she was sweeping his body, stroking his skin, twining her fingers in his hair.

'I love you, Dani,' he said raggedly, over and over. 'I love you. I've got to have you. I'm incomplete without you. Please!' he all but groaned. His hands got tangled up in her bathrobe and he fought it free, stripping it from her so she stood before him only in her nightgown. He seemed confused for a second, then he blinked dazed eyes and drew a little away to look down at her.

She was wearing nothing, but a long white nightgown of some thin material he could almost see through. It had a childish fringe of lace at the neck and her hair was loose and tumbling far down her back. Her eyes were wide and green and glittering and her feet were bare. All the colour left his face as he stood looking at her. Her lips were parted and glowing. Never had he seen her more beautiful.

'You look like a bride,' he said haltingly.

Brilliant colour ran up her neck.

'And the blush makes it perfect. You have been waiting for me all these years, haven't you, Dani? You'll be my wife now, won't you? You'll let me love you and care for you and look after you the rest of my life?'

Her breath strangled in the back of her throat and her mouth trembled and her heart hammered. Oh, how she wanted that. But could she? He was Ben, yet not Ben. Here in his arms everything was possible. And yet . . . She turned her face away.

He took her chin with unbearably gentle fingers. 'Look at me.'

Unwilling eyes lifted. 'I didn't think I'd ever hear you say those words to me, Ben.'

'I've waited a long time to say them.'

She couldn't help thinking of the past, of all the wasted time between them. She thought of Libby and his son and suddenly pictured that woman in the blue lace dress he was with earlier. They were worlds apart from her. His lifestyle was something she couldn't even begin to imagine. She shook her head from side to side, knowing it could never be. She winced as his fingers tightened on her chin. 'I can't marry you, Ben.'

He looked staggered. '*Why?* You love me. I know you do.' He pressed himself closer, wrapping his body around hers, his arms crushing her tightly to him. 'And you can feel how much I love you. Why?'

'We left it too late,' she muttered into his shoulder, her voice so quiet he could hardly hear it. 'We're different people now. You're wealthy——'

'Yes, I'm wealthy!' he exploded, stepping back and taking her hands in his. 'But my basics haven't changed. I'm still me. Just as you'll still be you once you start making all the money your painting will bring you. Don't you realise that?'

She kept looking at him, wanting to believe, yet her pride held her back. 'You think you have to be responsible for me, to take care of me.'

'I've always wanted to care for you. You know that. That's what love means to me.'

'There are others now.'

'Others? What others? Who?'

'Your son, for one.' Her whisper was choked. 'And . . . and . . .'

He blanched. His teeth clenched savagely. Something seemed to freeze up in him. 'And?'

'And that woman you were with tonight,' she ground out. 'She's very beautiful. So much more than I could ever be. You looked perfect together.'

His jaw sagged and his face reflected his astonishment. He tightened his hands on hers. 'What woman? You're the only woman I was with tonight.'

'At the University.'

He was at a total loss. 'I wasn't with any woman there.'

'You came in with her.'

His eyes widened then narrowed on her rapidly reddening face. 'You saw me come in? When I caught up to you in the parking lot, you said you were surprised to see me and you asked if I was just arriving. I was alone, Dani. What woman are you talking about?'

Her mouth shook. 'The one in the blue lace dress with the neckline down to here.'

He stopped dead and then a small smile began to twitch at the corners of his lips. 'Oh. That woman,' he almost chuckled.

She wanted to hit him. He was laughing at her and she knew it and it suddenly made her angry. 'Yes, that woman,' she said sarcastically.

'She was a beauty, wasn't she?'

Her breath caught harshly. How dare he?

'You're jealous!' he grinned boyishly, exultantly, lifting her up and almost swinging her around in his arms. 'That means you do care after all. Oh, Dani, you had me wondering.'

'Of course I care,' she lashed out. 'You're the most handsome man in the world. You know you can have your pick of any woman there is. Why do you waste your time with me?'

He laughed softly. 'My love, you're the only one who thinks so. I'm not wasting my time. I've loved you forever. There was never any choice about it. There's only you for me. I wasn't with that woman tonight. She happened to be coming in the same time I did. I remember stepping back at the door to let her go first. It was the polite thing to do, after all. She smiled prettily and thanked me and I couldn't help but notice how little there was of her dress. I'm human, you know, and I'm not blind. I don't know who she was, though. I was too intent on trying to find you. My father-in-law told me to be there tonight if I wanted to see what you really thought of me. I did see, Dani. That painting told me I hadn't lost you after all.

'What a gift you've got! You're fantastic! And so flattering. And you're still mine. You were always mine. And I'm yours.'

She swallowed the lump in her throat, wanting so desperately to believe him. But how could she? He was a different man from the one she had known. He was poised, assured, wealthy. She was still the same as she had been when he first met her all those years ago. He had gone on, grown, while she hadn't done anything. She was so plain. He was so handsome, so far above her.

'Will my son be a problem for you?' he asked softly.

She thought of the tiny baby she had last seen in the incubator in the hospital nursery. He would be a year and half old now. She wondered if he looked like Ben. 'I used to stand outside the glass and look at him and wish he was . . . ours.'

Relief swept through him. 'He is ours, my love. Libby gave him to us.' He smiled gently at her portrait. 'If she's somewhere looking down at us now, I'm sure she would approve. She would want you to be his mother. I haven't been much of a father up to now, but he's getting to the age where he needs both of us.'

Tears welled up in her eyes again and she felt deeply ashamed. 'Oh, Libby, I'm so sorry,' she said to the canvas.

'If you need forgiving, I'm sure she forgives you. Libby was that kind of person.' His arms closed around her tightly and he rested his chin on the top of her head. 'It took all this past year for your Mr Jones to convince me of that.'

'*My* Mr Jones?'

'Yours, my love. The way he talks about you, you're the daughter he lost. When I thought I'd ruined everything between us by turning away from you in the park, he told me all I had to do was bide my time until it all came right again. I used to doubt him. And sometimes I was so impatient. But he was right. He was, Dani, believe me. This is the right time for us.'

Oh, how she wanted to believe that. A small flame started deep inside her. 'And you, Ben? Can you forgive me?'

His face softened. He gently brushed away the tears dripping down her cheeks and smoothed her hair back away from her face, loving the way her skin was so flushed. There were red patches under her eyes and her lips were glowing and parted.

'Only if you promise to marry me.'

Their eyes locked. An aching tension spiralled through her as her fingers touched his mouth. She had done this so many times to his portrait, imagining him saying this to her. He was here now. He was real, flesh and blood, bone and sinew, and he wanted to marry her! Tracing the beautiful line of his lips, she delighted in his quickened breathing and trembled with a restless desperation. Her hands moved to his body with touching innocence, yet raw unappeasable hunger.

Never had she felt such a surge of desire for him, such an intensity that obliterated everything else until nothing mattered, but the final flaming consummation of that desire. He was Ben and he was hers. There was nothing to stop them now, not her mother or her poverty or her inadequacy, not his wife or his wealth or his pride. Nothing.

'Oh, Ben,' she got out on a strangled breath, wild excitement swamping her. 'I love you so very much. I want to marry you more than I ever wanted anything in my whole life.'

He sent a satisfied look to the canvas again and thought he saw a smile on the painted lips that wasn't there before then he looked back down to Danielle. 'I love you,' he said gently.

He stopped being gentle. The waiting was over. His kiss was hungry, fierce, passionate, his mouth blazing a trail of fire across the parted softness of her lips and down the long warm curve of her neck. He murmured incoherently, sounds of pleasure and relief.

She gloried in his trembling desire, in the sound and scent and feel of him, and matched his hunger with her own. Her arms mindlessly slid up around his neck, her hands eagerly invading the virile thickness of his hair, caressing the shape of his head, all her longing evident in her touch. Her whole being arched towards him, aching to know the thrusting demand of his hard body, to share at last the intimacies she had only imagined before.

No amount of imagination could have prepared her for the sensations he was arousing in her now. His mouth moved back and forth on her, warm and probing and insistent. She shivered uncontrollably when his hands cupped her bottom then began sliding surely up over her hips to her waist, his fingers probing the bones of her rib cage. When he reached the rounded contours of her swelling breasts and held them, stroking the hardened nipples through her thin nightgown, she trembled so violently she nearly fell.

'You're driving me crazy, do you know that?' he said huskily, his mouth still exploring hers.

Her hands were boldly sliding and bumping over his solid male shape, urged on by his murmurs of encouragement and praise. 'Oh, Ben. Ben!' her cry was almost incoherent. 'Love me! Please love me!'

She couldn't settle for anything less. Not now. There had to be the complete union of their bodies as well as their minds and hearts and souls.

But Ben still had a fingerhold on self-control. He took a deep breath and pulled himself together with an effort. Leaning a little away from her, he looked down at her glowing face and hungry eyes. A small smile moved across his lips. 'Not here, my love. Not now. But in our own bedroom after we're married.'

She looked crestfallen. How could he do this to her? Lead her this far and then stop?

'Mr Jones will be waiting for us,' he said softly.

'Mr Jones?' She blinked dazedly and suddenly remembered where she was.

He must have come home by now, although she hadn't heard him come in. Brilliant colour poured into her face. What had she been thinking? That was all she needed: to have him walk in on her while she was making mad passionate love to Ben. Thank God he had kept a sane head in all this. She tried to smile at him but failed miserably.

'Don't you think it strange that he's still not home after all this time?' he asked.

She couldn't understand what he was saying. He said Mr Jones was waiting for them, yet now he said he wasn't home.

Ben's hands kept stroking her back, tracing her hard bones and soft curves with warm heavy fingers, making her match his shudders of longing. Part of her wished he would stop while another part of her was afraid he would. He chuckled softly. 'He has a friend who's willing to perform our wedding ceremony tonight,' he said so gently she wanted to cry. 'He lives not too far away from here. He and Mr Jones go back a long way and since they're both night owls, they said they'd wait up for us no matter how long it took. I've had the licence for days now. All I needed was my bride. You don't mind if it's just us, do you? Or do you want to wait and have a proper wedding with all the trimmings and our families to wish us well?'

'You're the only one I ever wanted to be at my wedding, Ben,' she said breathlessly. 'If you're there, I wouldn't even be aware of any trimmings.'

He squeezed her tightly to him then flicked back his cuff and looked at his watch. 'Haven't we kept Mr Jones waiting long enough?'

She blushed brilliantly. 'You were that sure of me? Both of you?'

'Not sure, Dani. Just determined. If it took all night, I wasn't leaving here without you. You're mine. Mr Jones saw it in your painting. It'll be all nice and legal in a few minutes and then you'll never, ever, leave me again.'

'I'll never want to,' she said rosily, melting all over him.

They both glanced at his watch again. It was the right time.

 *Harlequin Romance*

Coming Next Month

2785   SOME SAY LOVE Lindsay Armstrong
Rescuing his late friend's daughter becomes habit-forming for
an Australian real-estate tycoon. So when she recklessly falls in
love with him, he marries her. But does he love her?

2786   PRISONER OF SHADOW MOUNTAIN
        Mariel Kirk
When a successful model regains consciousness after a plane
crash her mind is blank. She knows only that she's attracted to
her ruggedly handsome rescuer—despite the wedding band
found in her belongings!

2787   A GIRL NAMED ROSE Betty Neels
Quite by accident, a vacationing English staff nurse encounters
an impressive Dutch surgeon. And quite by surprise, she's
chosen to work with him, though he probably would have
preferred her pretty friend.

2788   HEARTBREAK PLAINS Valerie Parv
Australia's Chedoona Downs is a beautiful place to stay—even
as a virtual prisoner. But once her rich and powerful captor
discovers she's not the woman he's looking for, why won't he
let her go?

2789   MISLEADING ENCOUNTER Jessica Steele
When it's time to fall in love, a London model decides to
choose carefully. And the aggressive electronics company
owner love chooses for her doesn't seem a good choice at all.

2790   SWEET POISON Angela Wells
To conceal her sister's extramarital tryst, a young woman new
to Spain accepts dishonor—never dreaming she'll be forced
to marry the one man capable of exposing her lie...and
her innocence.

Available in September wherever paperback books are sold,
or through Harlequin Reader Service.

In the U.S.
P.O. Box 1397
Buffalo, N.Y.
14240-1397

In Canada
P.O. Box 2800, Postal Station A
5170 Yonge Street
Willowdale, Ontario M2N 6J3

Take 4 books
& a surprise gift
FREE

SPECIAL LIMITED-TIME OFFER

Mail to   **Harlequin Reader Service®**

In the U.S.
901 Fuhrmann Blvd.
P.O. Box 1394
Buffalo, N.Y. 14240-1394

In Canada
P.O. Box 2800, Station "A"
5170 Yonge Street
Willowdale, Ontario M2N 6J3

YES! Please send me 4 free Harlequin Presents® novels and my free surprise gift. Then send me 8 brand-new novels every month as they come off the presses. Bill me at the low price of $1.75 each ($1.95 in Canada)—a 11% saving off the retail price. There are no shipping, handling or other hidden costs. There is no minimum number of books I must purchase. I can always return a shipment and cancel at any time. Even if I never buy another book from Harlequin, the 4 free novels and the surprise gift are mine to keep forever.   116-BPR-BP6F

Name	(PLEASE PRINT)	

Address		Apt. No.

City	State/Prov.	Zip/Postal Code

This offer is limited to one order per household and not valid to present subscribers. Price is subject to change.   DOP-SUB-1R

HARLEQUIN HISTORICAL

Explore love with Harlequin in the Middle
Ages, the Renaissance, in the Regency, the
Victorian and other eras.

Relive within these books the endless ages of
romance, set against authentic historical
backgrounds. Two new historical love stories
published each month.

HISFA-1